LOST WOMEN
Banished Souls

LOST WOMEN
Banished Souls

STORIES BY
Garnett Kilberg Cohen

University of Missouri Press
Columbia and London

Copyright © 1996 by Garnett Kilberg Cohen
University of Missouri Press, Columbia, Missouri 65201
Printed and bound in the United States of America
All rights reserved
5 4 3 2 1   00 99 98 97 96

Library of Congress Cataloging-in-Publication Data

Cohen, Garnett Kilberg.
    Lost women, banished souls : stories / Garnett Kilberg
    Cohen.
        p. cm.
    ISBN 0-8262-1073-2 (alk. paper)
    1. Manners and customs—Fiction.   I. Title.
PS3553.04228L67   1996
813'.54–dc20   96-20494
                                                    CIP

∞ ™ This paper meets the requirements of the
American National Standard for Permanence of Paper
for Printed Library Materials, Z39.48, 1984.

Designer: Kristie Lee
Typesetter: BOOKCOMP
Printer and Binder: Thomson-Shore, Inc.
Typefaces: Giovanni, Mistral, Univers

For acknowledgments, see page 155.

To my parents, Mary and Vince,
and particularly to my son, Jim

Contents

From an Eyelash	1
Cousin Rina's Return	12
Wrongs	24
Guests	34
Burying the Dead	50
A Position of Trying	63
The Call of Private Ghosts	70
Aunts	84
Maps	99
Where You Can't Touch Bottom	110
Appetites	123
Fabric	130
Lost Women, Banished Souls	140

LOST WOMEN
Banished Souls

From an Eyelash

She was a child of anxious, not proud, love.
—Tillie Olsen, "I Stand Here Ironing"

The first page contains only a single photograph—a passport-sized black-and-white taken while Rebecca was still in the hospital, just hours after her birth. I look at it and remember.

When the nurse first carried Rebecca into my room, she was tightly bound in a well-worn pink blanket covered with little nubs. The nurse smiled and held her out to me.

"Do you want to count her toes?" she asked.

"No, no," I said. "Take her away." Then, not wanting to appear lacking in maternal instincts, I added, "I'm sure I'll want to look at everything on her later."

What a silly response! But the question was sillier. I couldn't imagine unbinding those limbs to flop without restraint, exposing all her pink skin to the atmospheric germs, simply to count toes. Wouldn't they tell me if she had a missing one or an extra one? Did they think I didn't trust them? Or were they practical jokers? In my mind's eye I saw the staff out in the hall, a huddle of starched uniforms, laughing and nudging each other, whispering, "Wait till *this* mother gets a load of her kid's deformed toes."

After the nurse departed, the woman in the other bed, a hill woman who had migrated from West Virginia to Ohio for factory work, said, "When they brang me my baby, I'm sure as hell gonna look at them toes." Although she had delivered almost two hours after me, she was already sitting straight up against her pillows, ratting her red hair, checking her face from all angles in her dirty pearl-colored hand mirror.

She was true to her word. She grabbed her infant daughter from the nurse's arms and removed the baby blanket as unceremoniously as if she were unwrapping a ham sandwich.

An amateur talent show was on the television hooked to our ceiling. Three seven-year-old girls—with painted faces, permed hair, and sequined bathing suits—were attempting to tap in unison. My roommate, Mavis, I think her name was, glanced up at the screen and said, "My girl's gonna be a dancer."

Then, to my horror, Mavis began dancing her naked infant around the bed like a plucked chicken, using only the cup of her right hand as a brace for the wobbling head. A trace of spittle trailed from the infant's mouth.

"On the good ship Lolly Pop. Da-da-da daaa da-da da. On the good ship Lolly Pop," Mavis sang out of tune, her head wagging back and forth as she hopped her baby about.

I considered protesting, but decided against it; she had more experience than me. In the three hours we'd shared the room, I'd learned she was on her second marriage (a statistic that seemed beyond comprehension to me at the time) and had two natural sons and two stepsons. Surely she knew what she was doing.

"I can't believe how lucky I am!" Mavis said. "I prayed so hard for a girl child while I was on the table that I wouldn't be surprised if God up and changed her sex right then and there when she popped her head out."

My literal self wondered, if that were so, whether or not little Tiffany would have questions about her sexual identity. Somehow, I knew not to mention this to Mavis.

A minute later I was again horrified when Mavis pressed Tiffany down on the bed and spread open her stubby little legs.

"Finally! I get to see some girl parts. I'm so sick of all them penises."

I had laughed, thinking how I would tell the story to my husband, David, and our friends. I never did. Probably because I didn't trust myself to use an honest tone. I imagined I would sound mocking or condescending, when in reality, as stunned as I was, I actually admired the woman: her imperviousness, and even more important, her ability to envision the future. My life has never fanned out before me in possibilities; instead, it trails behind like the series of photos in this album. I couldn't imagine Rebecca tap-dancing at age seven. In fact, I couldn't imagine her any older than a toddler. Was my lack of vision some sort of prophecy?

I never did unwrap Rebecca's blanket in the hospital or relax when they brought her for nursing. Instead, I would tightly clutch her—terrified that she would roll off the bed, choke to death, or smother in all the blankets—waiting impatiently for the nurse's return. The images of her demise were countless, and so vivid that I could even hear the sound of her skull cracking against the clean hospital floor. Never would I have guessed that I wouldn't even be present for her death, that it would come just as I was beginning to trust in her resilience when she was almost five years old. Nor would I have imagined her demise would be the result of something as prosaic as a middle-aged woman running a red light in order to get home to check on a pot roast. I always felt Rebecca was safe when she was with David. It was just my care I mistrusted.

Once more, I look at the photograph. All the affection I denied Rebecca as a newborn, I lavished on that photo. In the hospital, I kept it under my pillow. When Rebecca wasn't actually clutched in my anxious embrace, I held that photo in the frame of my fingertips, marveling at the patch of dark hair that later turned blond, studying the perfectly formed features, and wondering how such a creature could have issued from my womb.

The soft, frayed photo edges testify to my constant touch.

I take a sip of the tea on the table next to me, rest my head against the wicker rocker back, and close my eyes. Odd that I preferred the photograph to my real living, breathing baby, and odder still that now I must use the photograph to extract memories of my real baby.

I open my eyes and glance at Rebecca's footprints on the opposite page. The hospital staff printed them while she was still in their nursery. I wonder how. Did they press the ink pad and book against her feet, rolling the pages against her curled toes as she lay on her belly? Or did they stand her up, first on the ink pad, then on the book? I smooth the page with my open palm before turning it.

The next page spread is what makes the album so bulky. I taped it full of souvenirs. A lock of her fine infant hair tied in a pink satin ribbon. A small plastic bag containing the remnants of her first nail clippings—yellowing like old rice kernels. Our hospital bracelets— laminated paper in plastic, so different from the lovely little beaded one (with a bead for each letter) that I had as an infant. Newspaper headlines from the Akron, Ohio, daily clipped on the day she was born. A postcard of the hospital that looks as if it was printed twenty years before Rebecca's birth.

I almost laugh when I see the photographs on the next page. One is of Chloe, David, Rebecca, and me, right after I'd returned from the hospital. David is sitting on one side of me, Chloe on the other, and Rebecca is on my lap. We are all—Rebecca included—wearing disposable surgical masks. I had brought them home from the hospital, foolishly planning to ask everyone to don one before handling Rebecca. How had I imagined that my cynical young husband or my worldly best friend would go along with such a rule? The photograph was snapped by Moji, the man Chloe would marry soon afterward. She is wearing a black blouse with long sleeves, a long black skirt, and no makeup, in deference to Moji's Arab customs. Who would have guessed how much things would change? That Chloe and Moji would have married and divorced? That David and Rebecca would have lived and died?

The other photo is of David wearing an enormous cup of my nursing bra on his head, aviator-cap style, leaving the other cup and the straps to trail down his back. He looks so jolly, so irreverent, so unsuspecting. I want to kiss his bruised eyes. I remember him soaring through the apartment, his arms outstretched like airplane wings, and this time I do laugh out loud. My laugh, the only noise in my small house, sounds lost and plaintive.

I turn the pages. For the first year, page after page painstakingly records every detail of Rebecca's life. Her first words. Her first steps. Her first Christmas gifts. All in my neat, careful script. Cards she received. And more photographs. These photos are all colored, yellowing now with age. Some were taken by David. Some by me. And others at the temporary stands Sears erected every few months. Rebecca seated on a dingy patch of shag carpeting with a backdrop of blue skies and bulbous Renaissance-type clouds. Rebecca on a fake swing placed on blue felt with another blue sky backdrop.

She is a thin child, but not unusually thin. I study her face—the eyes enormous and bruised like David's eyes, the cleft in her chin like mine, the high forehead, the translucent, faintly mottled skin—for signs of fragility, of disease before I remind myself (as I sometimes need to do) that she didn't die of a long illness, but in a car accident. I couldn't have known what was coming. No physician or advanced diagnosis would have been able to prolong her life.

Sometime after her first year, the album becomes less meticulously maintained—as if I had given up. Except for a crayon drawing folded and inserted in between pages, the middle of the album is completely empty. I open the drawing, careful not to break the brittle paper along the fold, and look at the picture. She must have been close to four when she drew it. The shapes and lines are carefully rendered, an interesting composition of abstract images in primary colors. I'm reminded of a Kandinsky. Only I can see the shapes are functioning in some way—what way, I'll never know. I wonder why it was the only drawing of hers I saved. Did it have some special meaning? Now it does—it is the only thing she ever created that has survived.

Once more, I sip my tea. Outside a gentle snow dots the sky, yet the trees are thick with the snow from the previous night's heavy fall. The branches are so weighted that the trees look like fabulous big plumes plucked from the Three Musketeers' grand hats. Beyond my front porch posts and the houses across the way, the sun is setting. Between the obstructions, the lavender clouds stretch in layers sandwiched between strips of pale peach sky, reminding me of textbook illustrations of the earth's sediments.

I skip to the back of the album where there are more photographs, and I remember that I had not actually given up recording Rebecca's life, but, in fact, our old camera had broken. We didn't replace it until we went to Maine.

I've labeled these photographs "Our First Family Vacation." A friend of David's parents had loaned us their ski home in Maine (a small gesture since it was in western Maine and abandoned during the summer anyway). We'd camped twice during the trip there, but only made occasional pit stops during the nineteen-hour drive home. (David told me his father never stopped on car trips, so they had to pee in a coffee can.) I'd read all of *Anna Karenina* in the car while David drove.

There are photographs of people we met during the trip. (No one stayed in the vacation houses surrounding us—a little ski village— since it was deserted for the summer. But we made day trips.) These eclectic shots are much clearer. Our new camera focused sharply on the central image, and left the background watery. I don't remember the name of the first man we photographed. He is a handsome man from New York who'd told David that whenever he ended a relationship with a woman, he disappeared into the depths of the subway and didn't emerge until he had a date with a new woman. His latest subway acquisition is hanging from his arm. We took their address and promised to send them a print. We never did. Next to it is a photograph of an eight-year-old boy who befriended Rebecca on the beach. He is making a castle in the sand as Rebecca watches. Then there is a folksinger with hair to his waist on a street corner. We gave him a dollar. He told us not to lose the photograph since he would one day be famous. Of course, I have never heard of him since. There is a lobster boat captain in a yellow raincoat even though the sky behind him is clear blue. For the tourists, I guess. For us. My favorite shot is of the vacation village, taken from a ski slope at sundown. There are two dozen houses, yet ours is the only one occupied, the only one with lights. The image brings back the eerie feeling I had whenever we walked through the village, as if we were the only family on earth.

On the next page, I've recorded our obligatory lobster dinner. The cauldron boiling on the stove. David looking impish as he salts the water. Our three live lobsters standing at attention on the kitchen counter. Rebecca holding the pinched face of her lobster close to the camera so that her fingertips are much bigger and clearer than her face. I remember how she played with that lobster, as if it were a toy car, racing it around the kitchen floor with her hand. She tried to rev it up by winding her thin right arm around and around before releasing the poor animal. She let it go with a flourish as if she'd created a momentum that would propel the lobster across the floor. Of course it only skidded a short distance. After she had tired of the car game, she dressed the lobster like a little doll. She used a napkin as a cape and made a paper hat.

When it was finally time to drop her lobster in the pot, she had paused for just a moment, holding the lobster over the bubbling water, shut her eyes, and whispered "I love you" before she let it go.

After our vacation, there are no more photographs until Thanksgiving. And even then, there is only one. David cutting the turkey, a deceptively healthy looking bird. David's unsuspecting parents, who had driven up from North Carolina that morning, are sitting on either side of him. (At the time, I'd wondered if they had been able to make the trip in half a day because his staid mother had abided by the family custom of peeing in a coffee can.) I had taken the fourteen-pound bird out of the freezer at 9 A.M. thinking that, like a pound of hamburger, it would thaw by noon. When it was still as hard as a rock at eleven, we had filled the bathtub with hot water and stuck the bird in it, taking turns holding it beneath the surface with David's old baseball bat. I still remember my frustration whenever the bird had slipped free and popped to the surface.

The three final photographs were taken during David and Rebecca's last Christmas. Rebecca dressed in a red velvet empire-waisted dress with a white lace collar—the type I'd imagined little girls should wear at Christmas. Behind her is a blur of colored lights and pine needles. Rebecca, in fuzzy yellow pajamas with feet, opening a box wrapped in silver paper. I no longer remember what was inside. David showing mock surprise at whatever is inside a box as big as a television set. I don't remember what it contained either. What I do remember happened two weeks later, just a week before Rebecca and David were killed.

David and I had been reading in the living room when all of a sudden a horrible scream came from Rebecca's room. I'd dropped my book and run to her bed. David followed me. I remember his silhouette in the doorway. I'd knelt beside her. "What is it Rebecca? Tell me. What's the matter?" Her lip was trembling and her eyes were wide with horror. She shook her head back and forth violently. "I'm going to die," she said. "I plugged in the Christmas tree, after I got out of the bath, I plugged it in." At first I had no idea what she was talking about. The tree had been down for a week, the ornaments packed away. "Mommy, I'm going to be electrocuted." And then as the realization hit me, I sighed with relief. I had told her never to plug in the tree without me there, particularly if she was wet, because she could be electrocuted and die. "Rebecca," I asked, "when did you plug the tree in?" She was sobbing. "The day before we threw it away. Daddy had just dried me off and put my pj's on." She obviously didn't realize the two things were so immediately connected. She thought she could die later, the way a smoker dies from cancer. I'd smiled at David's dark form in the doorway. "It's okay," I said. "Never mind." When he disappeared, I stroked Rebecca's brow, "No, no, baby, you can't die now. It can only happen *when* you plug the tree in. If it didn't happen then, you're safe. But I want you to promise me you'll never plug anything else in without asking me first." She shook her head. I stayed with her until she fell asleep. Later, when I told David what she thought, we had both laughed. Yet Rebecca had been right. She was going to die, both she and her father.

I close the album. My tea is cold. And the living room is almost dark. In the fading gray light, I can only discern shapes, no details. I don't feel like switching on a lamp. Instead, I think of the way we laughed. Never could we have imagined such a coincidence, such bad luck. If bad *luck* it was. Perhaps it was good luck. Perhaps I was lucky to have over four years with her. She could have been a stillborn, died of crib death, or died of a lingering disease. Perhaps I am lucky to have such happy memories of David. Maybe he would have grown fat and bald and sexless, finally leaving me for another woman. Or maybe he would have become bitter and we would have turned into two old people left with nothing to say to one another. Could he have overcome his guilt if he had lived and she had died? Would I have been able to bury mine?

Rebecca died in the same hospital where she was born. I hadn't been there since her birth. At that time I was so groggy I don't even remember who told me she was a girl. But I remember everything about the physician who told me she was dying, right down to the very pores on his nose. I can still recall the angle of his mouth as he told me David had died on impact, but not to worry, there was still hope—Rebecca was still alive.

"Hanging by an eyelash, but alive," he said.

I looked beyond the purple pores on his shiny nose, up to his eyes, to see a tiny eyelash resting on his cheekbone. How ironic, I wanted to say, you've just mentioned "eyelash" and there's one on your cheek. Or is this some sort of visual aid? A demonstration of what a tenuous attachment an eyelash can be? I almost laughed as I imagined him carefully plucking an eyelash and sticking it to his cheek before he left the operating room to talk to me. But before a hint of hysteria could escape my lips, my literal self took over and I imagined Rebecca, my beautiful Rebecca, in a soft angel's robe with sweeping feathery white wings, clutching an enormous eyelash. In my mind's eye, I saw her hanging there—the pink soles of her feet kicking wildly—suspended above a vast nothingness, and I was powerless to help her.

It was only twenty minutes later when the same doctor, now faceless and poreless, returned to tell me she was gone. *Gone? How could she possibly have gotten out of the hospital?* And then it hit me. She was dead too. I didn't need to worry about her at all anymore. Then came the slump of my shoulders. The sigh of relief. It was over. She was free. I was free. Neither of us had to depend on my incompetence any longer. What mother could feel such a thing? What mother could feel relief?

I flip back to the first page and look at the hospital black-and-white of Rebecca. In the dim light, I can see nothing, but still I think of her as an infant, and think of Mavis and her daughter, Tiffany, how Mavis believed herself capable, so therefore she was. How she believed she was lucky simply because her child was a girl. Maybe that was it—you were what you believed, capable or incapable, lucky or unlucky, regardless of what happened to you. Perhaps I should have put more stock in what Mavis said. It's too late now, but if Rebecca were alive, I would call the hospital, try to trace Mavis. I'm sure the search wouldn't be difficult—how far could she have gone from the hills of southern Ohio?

When I got her on the telephone line, I would request a reunion. Someone who makes her own luck would never say no to such a suggestion.

I can imagine the four of us in her living room. Outside the boys (whose penises Mavis was sick of looking at), all in their late teens or early twenties now, would be working on old Chevies jacked up on cinder blocks. The yard would be a series of crisscrossed tire tracks, but Mavis, lucky Mavis, master of her own fate, would still have managed to do something creative with what she had. Perhaps there would be a colorful fence made out of various old car hoods, all jammed in the ground side by side. Or maybe she would have spray painted a bunch of old tires and used them as planters. Regardless, inside it would be just us women, amid the clutter—walls covered with tap-dancing plaques and shelves crowded with tap trophies stuffed with plastic flowers.

"Let me get you all a bite. Just a little something I threw together for the occasion," Mavis would say before fluttering off to the kitchen, and returning with cherry Kool-Aid and a cherry Jell-O mold. "I put marshmallows and pretzels in the Jell-O because that's how my baby likes it." Then she would pinch Tiffany's cheek and say, "Show 'em your stuff, girl."

Next, Tiffany, a chubby fourteen year old in a magenta sequined bathing suit with fringe above the crotch, and matching sequined shoes, would step into the middle of our circle of overstuffed armchairs, and tap and twirl for us. I can see her smiling, beaming in fact, alternating marching with tap, the baton serving as a tap cane one minute and a majorette's instrument the next. She struts and taps. Struts and taps. Then tosses the baton in the air. All our eyes follow. Mavis nods knowingly. Again and again, the baton flies up. Ohhhh. Ahhhh. What talent! Each toss sails higher in the air until finally the ceiling must stretch to accommodate it. The room swells and begins pulsating to marching band music that has erupted out of nowhere. We all cheer. The sequins on Tiffany's belly oscillate like rippling water. The baton twirls higher, higher, higher, until the ceiling opens up to make way for the silver rod. We all watch as it spins off into the robin's-egg-blue heavens. We all take one long, final gasp of breath before Tiffany sinks back in her chair, triumphant.

Mavis takes a bite of cherry Jell-O and says, "So, what does your girl do?" One small quivering sliver of Jell-O remains on her lower lip.

I look at Rebecca expectantly. We all do, though I am most curious. Her face has not aged any since she was four, yet her body has grown. She shuffles in her seat, as if still getting accustomed to her fourteen-year-old body. What would she do? Surely not twirl. Perhaps she would be a person of paper, bringing life to flat surfaces, writing, drawing, even origami—what do I care? As long as she does *something*. Then I notice her face is pale, so pale that I can't distinguish her features. She is fading. Fading and shrinking. She is smaller than when we arrived, and getting smaller. Her little legs are a four year old's now, not even long enough to dangle over the edge of the chair. She is like a doll, a translucent doll, posed in the chair, her stiff limbs sticking straight out. And then she is gone.

I realize that not even Mavis can grant me impunity.

"She dies, Mavis," I say. "Over and over again, every day of my life, she dies. That's what she does, Mavis."

Like most cold tea, mine tastes bitter now. The house is deathly quiet. And my living room is completely dark. The only illumination comes from the front window where outside the gentle blue-white snowflakes, like the feathery remnants of a heavenly explosion, gracefully drift to earth.

Cousin Rina's Return

My mother didn't like visiting Uncle Richard, Aunt Naomi, Rina, and the boys. She never said it, but I knew. My mother was a bit of a snob. We talked to her family weekly and we visited them on important holidays like Christmas and Thanksgiving, as well as a few weeks every summer. We only saw Daddy's brother Richard's family two or three days a year on the leftover holidays—maybe Memorial Day or Labor Day, and once on the Fourth of July.

Short as those visits were, I loved them. Uncle Richard's family was different from anyone we knew in our regular life in Chicago. Uncle Richard and Aunt Naomi both dyed their hair a matching bluish black. So did Rina, their daughter who was four years older than me. Rina's brothers—Clay, Clint, and Randy—were all towheads but I imagined they would coat their flaxen locks when they got older. It was a family tradition (the same way my mother's mother put four different forks with the family monogram "P" at each place for Thanksgiving and Christmas dinners). The black hair brought out Naomi's and Rina's pale skin and almond eyes, which were slightly slanted. Though Naomi had moved up to Indiana from Tennessee where she (and at least three generations before her) had been born, both she and her daughter looked strangely exotic, almost Asian, particularly Rina. Her face was so round and flat that her nose was no more than a bubble on her profile. She ratted her black hair up in a bouffant, fluffing it out around her face like flower petals. At fourteen, she wore false eyelashes and dark black eyeliner, drawn out in the corners like a geisha girl. She told me that when she turned twenty-one she planned to have her eyes operated on to make them look Oriental; with the balls of her hands, she shoved back her temples to demonstrate the full effect. She was always nice to me, treated me like an equal her own age. I thought both she and her mother were glamorous.

At fourteen, Rina already had a grown-up figure like her mother's: tiny, but curvaceous. They were like two miniature hourglasses, waists as small as Tinker Bell's or Wilma Flintstone's. But Rina stomped around barefoot in a way that made her presence seem larger than it actually was.

Their front yard was magical. Although they lived right outside South Bend, they had decorated their front lawn in a mix of Asian and west Tennessee icons. Fed with all kinds of chemicals, their grass was a brilliant toxic green. Smack in the middle, beneath a weeping willow, was a lily pond containing goldfish the size of my father's shoes. An arched bridge, strong enough to support me until I was ten, curved over the blue-green water. Like mini oases, clumps of flowers were planted randomly around the yard. In the center of each clump was a little statue, a replica of either a miniature plantation or an eight-tiered pagoda. Near the base of the bridge on the willow side were life-size ceramic statues of Rhett Butler and Scarlett O'Hara. Naomi had painted the white molded forms herself so that both Rhett's and Scarlett's lips looked a little too red and garish, as if each of them was half movie star and half vampire. But from the distance they looked like real people. Tied to a dozen or so of the sweeping willow branches were baskets stuffed with artificial flowers. And hidden in various spots around the yard were plastic butterflies and ceramic squirrels. The yard took my breath away!

Rina and I often reclined under the willow, talking, curling our toes in the vivid green grass. We had a special privacy there. (Clint, Clay, and Randy weren't allowed in the front yard and I had no siblings.) Once after we had spent a languid hour lying on our backs looking up at the swaying baskets, Rina painting my fingernails the color of a seashell's pink lining, I was so overcome with emotion that I ran into the kitchen where my mother and Aunt Naomi (Rina called her mother "Ma") were drinking coffee.

"Mother, oh Mother," I said. "When we get home can we fix up our front yard just like Aunt Naomi and Uncle Richard's?"

Aunt Naomi looked pleased, but my mother looked annoyed. She was wearing a knit navy suit with white piping. Her hair was subtly frosted. She had perfect posture, yet she managed to sit up even straighter in her chair in response to my inquiry.

"I don't think that would be possible, dear," said my mother, flashing me a tight-lipped smile that I'd already come to recognize as her quintessential snob smile, meant to terminate conversation. But I was both crestfallen and irritated by the way that my mother looked so obviously bored and stoic, taken with her own ability to endure such a visit, so I pressed on.

"Why not? Can't we afford it?"

My mother looked horror-struck. Discussion of money was our family's strictest taboo.

"We will discuss it later," she said.

The next day, on the ride back to Chicago, I got both a lecture on inappropriate subject matter as well as a detailed definition of what the word *tacky* meant. She made "tacky" seem like a necessary evil that we had to tolerate at times, as a matter of kindness, but certainly nothing that we would ever *like*. I worried for a while that there might be something wrong with me, because if my regard for the garden was any indication, I was definitely prone toward the tackier things in life. But it didn't really matter. The yard was just a symbol. What I really envied and admired was their lifestyle and behavior.

Rina and her brothers were permitted so many things I was denied: fast food, limitless television, cheese curls that left their fingertips orange, and cherry soda pop. They stayed outside well past dark, and could set off their own fireworks on the Fourth of July. I was never even allowed to purchase any fireworks besides babyish sparklers. And while they were no more religious than my parents, Naomi did come from Southern Baptist roots. She was extremely superstitious and respected all the folklore from her Tennessee childhood. Naomi's mother was actually known to speak in tongues, a phenomenon that Rina demonstrated for me by convulsing and rolling about on the cartoon-green grass, babbling at an indecipherable speed, her eyes turned back so far that just the flickering whites showed.

I only met Rina's maternal grandparents once, during our one and only visit to South Bend on the Fourth of July. They had driven up from Tennessee for the holiday. They were the oldest looking couple

I'd ever seen, their dried-apple faces crisscrossed with so many tiny straight lines and creases that their noses and mouths got lost in the patterns. Their glittering black eyes looked like chips of flint pressed into leather. The old woman wore a shapeless flowered shift to her knees and the old man wore a tank-top undershirt (I'd never seen such elderly collapsed male muscles) and a red duck-billed hat poked with fishing hooks and lures. Richard constantly argued with the old man about religion. I remember part of a conversation they had about Heaven. Richard asked why, if Heaven was a tangible place, didn't the astronauts run into it on their flights into space? The old man smiled serenely, leaned forward, wrists on his knees, and countered, "Did you ever think Heaven might be *inside* the moon?" He crossed his arms and sat back in his seat, very pleased with himself.

My mother, erect on the edge of a La-Z-Boy recliner, rolled her eyes, an unusual breach of etiquette for her.

"Don't question what you don't know," the old lady said, her black eyes shining.

"Wait," I said, seriously trying to understand. "I don't get it, isn't the stuff you don't know the stuff you're supposed to question?"

"Ann," my father said to me. "Why don't you go outside with the other kids."

"No," my mother said. "They're doing fireworks."

"Oh, let her have some fun," said Aunt Naomi. "The kids are real careful."

"I'm sure they are," said my mother in that tactful, tolerant way she had. "But Ann isn't accustomed to fireworks. *She* might make a mistake."

So I was allowed to stay inside and listen to these strange old folks from Tennessee talk in thick accents about the location of the trapdoor in the moon, haunted houses, friends they knew who'd talked to Jesus, southern cures (my favorite was standing knee-deep in a creek during a full moon; I don't recall the nature of the ailment), the time the old woman had an out-of-body experience, how Rina was born with a web over her face that meant she could see things other people couldn't, and recipes for squirrel and vine-ripe tomatoes. And all of this while the exploding firecrackers outside encroached. We were surrounded by bangs, pops, and fizzles. My mother claimed a headache and retired early, and my father and

Richard went out on the porch to watch the festivities and talk sports. But I stayed up listening to stories until Rina and her brothers came inside, smelling of gunpowder and smoke. Rina had a smudge of ashes across her cheek.

"Jesus," said Rina. "I wish you could've seen it, Annie."

"Don't call the son of the Lord's name unless you know what you want to ask him," said the old woman.

"Huh?" asked Clay.

"How would you like it if he showed up in person this very instant and all Rina had to tell him about was fireworks?" snarled the woman as if she was sick of explaining such things to her imbecile grandchildren.

We pondered the possibility for a moment before Rina and the boys told me about all the fireworks I had missed. A cherry bomb had gone off just seconds after Clint had tossed it. A bottle rocket had exploded on the ground, searing the grass three feet in every direction. They had hurled firecrackers in the next door neighbors' pond. A tree branch had caught fire from a Roman candle. My cousins were so excited in their narrations that they were jumping around, interrupting each other. The night sounded wonderfully exciting. My chest grew tight at the thought of missing so much adventure. Apparently Rina sensed that I felt excluded, because she asked her mother if she could show me Aunt Naomi's jewelry. Naomi went and got her enormous satin jewel box from her bedroom. Then, everyone but Rina and me went to bed. Rina and I sat up trying on the tangle of opal rings, bangle bracelets, rhinestone earrings, and brooches. They were so different from my mother's few simple pieces and pearls that they fascinated me. I liked sitting next to Rina, watching her expressive face as she told tales, smelling the smoke in her hair. We talked and laughed until it was light outside. We were still sitting there when the old people got up for church. They asked us if we wanted to go, and we said yes. It never occurred to me that my parents might object. Although we were Episcopalian, they had twice let me go to church with friends back in Chicago, once to a Methodist service and another time to the Presbyterian church.

We went to a place the old folks visited every time they came up to Indiana. The service was wonderful, a revival meeting in a big tent. There must have been a thousand people. No one spoke in tongues, but a cripple was cured—actually threw away his crutches—

two people were baptized by being shoved fully clothed under water in a plastic wading pool, and, when called, dozens of people streamed down the aisle to the makeshift stage to be saved. All of these wonders were accompanied by four women in long red velvet dresses—though it must have been close to eighty degrees—singing Praise Jesus songs. The service ended at noon and the old people took us to Kentucky Fried Chicken for lunch.

When we got back to Rina's, my parents were waiting on the porch. I have never seen them so angry. My mother literally snatched me away from Rina's side, shoved me in our car's backseat, and slammed the door. The suitcases were already inside. My mother climbed in the front, while my father marched over to the old people. I was mortified by my parents' rudeness.

"Mother," I hissed. "You're embarrassing Rina's grandparents."

"They should be embarrassed," said my mother loud enough for them to hear since the car windows were down.

"Mother!"

"It was we who were wronged," she said.

My father, his face flushed crimson, said something I couldn't make out in a hushed and angry voice to the old people, then joined us in the car.

"They never should have taken you to such a place without our permission," said my mother, as if they had taken me to a porn film. That was the last thing said on the ride home. And our last visit to Uncle Richard's for nearly two years.

My father still talked to his brother on the phone and Rina sent me Christmas gifts: a manicure set one year and a collection of eight lipsticks in graduated colors of pink and white that I wasn't allowed to wear the following year. During that time of estrangement, I once asked my mother how my father and Richard could be brothers, yet be so different. Her answer surprised me.

"Oh, I don't know that they're really so different," she said. "I think it's just that they married very different women."

I thought about this for a while and decided my mother had probably given herself too much credit. My father, a tall man who usually wore a gray suit to work, would *never* dye his hair black. He chose his wife because of the way he turned out, not the other way around. What were small differences between my father and his brother when they were boys probably became big differences because of choices they made when they were eighteen. Since their mother (Granny Bryze who visited us from Florida every two years) was widowed young, she wasn't able to do anything for either son when they finished high school. My father chose to work his way through college, where he met my mother. Richard chose the army, where he met Naomi while stationed in Tennessee. It was that simple.

When we finally did visit Uncle Richard's family again, it was our last visit ever. We went for Granny Bryze's funeral. After visiting us in Chicago, she had taken Amtrak to South Bend to visit them. While there, she had suffered a fatal stroke.

Overall, everything at their house was the same, but individual things had changed. Naomi and Richard no longer had matching hair. His was still black, but hers was fire-hydrant red. I noticed that the children had poor grammar and even Naomi used double negatives. Clint had blown up his right hand when he failed to toss a cherry bomb in time. Three of the fingers had fused so that they looked like wads of chewed bubble gum stuck together; the two intact fingers stuck out of the glob like rabbit ears. He showed me how he could strike a match, flip eggs, and swing a bat, all with the deformed hand. I was fourteen and attending a private high school. The yard was still the same, but looked tacky to me now. I wished I'd never seen it again.

The biggest change was Rina. She was stunning in her beauty. If Naomi had looked anything like Rina at eighteen, I was not surprised that Uncle Richard had fallen in love with her—even though she wasn't quite "our kind." No longer ratted, Rina's hair hung in gentle waves to her waist. Her skin was flawless. Her eyes shone like polished stones.

And she was pregnant—an unwed mother with a belly as swollen as a watermelon. Her finely curved arms and legs were still slender, but her midsection was so huge that she had to carefully lower herself into chairs and be hoisted out of them.

My mother never once mentioned the pregnancy. But Naomi discussed it constantly. She had done a gender-determination test— adding Rina's urine to a cup of Drano (it was a boy); made strange concoctions for Rina to drink; and, most peculiar of all, she grabbed Clay's newborn baby puppy out of Rina's arms, saying it could mark the baby. She told us about a person in Tennessee whom everyone called the Mole Man because, as a result of his mother handling a mole during her pregnancy, he had come out resembling one. Because of other superstitions, she wouldn't dream of letting Rina attend Granny's funeral; it was bad enough that Rina had been in the house when she died. So Rina stayed home with me. Of course, I wasn't allowed to go.

I was glad to see that once we were alone, our rapport resumed right where it had left off. I stretched out on her pink chenille bedspread and we talked and we talked. Or rather, she talked and I listened. She told me how she was deeply in love with Ray, the baby's father, how he was a stock-car driver, how they were kindred spirits, and how she had kept the news of the baby from him so that he could proceed untethered with his career. I thought she was strong and brave. Stomping around the room, gesturing wildly, she described to me what it was like making love. She said it was as if you were completely empty inside except for a balloon, and every time the man pushed, he pumped the balloon out, fuller and fuller, until it filled your whole insides up, and the walls of the balloon were so thin that they burst—at this point Rina swept her arms around her head in wide frantic circles—sending out millions of rays of balloon skin to the very tips of your fingers, the tips of your toes, and right up behind your eyes to your scalp.

Wow, I thought.

Rina made us a lemonade and chip-n-dip snack in the special blue and red matching glass chip-n-dip bowls Naomi had. Of course by then I knew that such bowls were in poor taste, but I loved the order of it—having matching bowls for products that I wasn't even allowed to eat at home. After eating an entire bag of Charlie's Chips (the kind of chips delivered right to your home in a big tin canister), Rina made me a banana split in one of her mother's oblong banana boat bowls. I watched the look of concentration on her face—the delicate features of the flat surface pulled together, the bubble nose, the rosebud lips—as she sliced the banana. Standing there in the rays of golden twilight seeping through the chiffon kitchen curtains, her hair cascading in gentle ropes to her waist, Rina looked like an angel. By the time she topped my ice cream with nuts, the kitchen was growing dark. Instead of turning on any lights, Rina and I went into the TV room and put her orange lava lamp in the middle of the floor's orange shag carpeting. Ritualistically, we sat on either side while I ate my concoction, as if we were divided by a strange and bubbling campfire.

My parents, Naomi and Richard, and the boys all returned from the funeral right as we were finishing the dishes. Rina was wiping her tiny hands on a green and orange striped dish towel, thin wrists buried in the fabric, when we said good-bye.

About two weeks later I was reading in the rocking chair in my father's study when the phone rang. Even though it sat less than three feet away on my father's desk, I didn't get up to answer it. I had just reached a good part. My mother walked briskly past me—her lips pursed, tisk, tisk (we weren't on good terms)—and pulled the receiver from its carriage. Since I was deep in the book, I heard the conversation as if it was coming from a vast distance.

"Uh-huh. Uh-huh. Oh my God! Nooooo. *People simply don't do that anymore.* Yes, of course. Call me back as soon as you can."

At the same time that I felt my mother was only commenting on some horrible faux pas an acquaintance had committed, I was vaguely aware that something really terrible had happened.

My mother hung up the phone and looked at me.

"That was your father on the phone. Rina is dead. She died in childbirth."

I closed my book, but continued rocking, staring at my mother. Then my mother did something I had never seen her do before. Her face crumbled and she burst into tears. Without thinking, I rose and took her in my arms. As I held her, I remembered that she hadn't always been cold. A long-forgotten memory returned to me: when I was a tiny girl, my mother had rocked me in her arms and sung lullabies softly in my ear. I held her tighter and pictured her as an old woman, frail in my embrace; I pictured Rina as a nine year old standing on her bicycle pedals, her legs in a V as she coasted down an Indiana hill. I saw the gleam of the knife in the setting sun as Rina leaned, poised over the banana, making a perfect slit. I saw her wiping her hands on the dish towel. I saw all of us as we are, as we were, and as we will be—fragile and fearful and mortal. But all that I felt and saw was over so quickly that I couldn't begin to understand it.

I wasn't surprised when I wasn't permitted to go to the funeral. My mother said in her new, postembrace pragmatic/kind voice that she would rather have me remember Rina gay and alive than pale and stiff in a coffin. I never saw Rina's little boy. He was put up for adoption. And I didn't see Aunt Naomi again for many years. She had a breakdown, claimed Rina's ghost was visiting her at night. But for the following year, I envisioned Rina nearly daily, sometimes in her pink bedroom, sometimes in her mother's kitchen, sometimes in the 7-Up-bottle-green grass of her front lawn, but as often as not in the way my mother had planted her image in my head—stiff and pale in her coffin.

After that year, I thought of Rina less and less until it took a special encounter or occasion to trigger my memory. By the time I was twenty-seven and having my first child, Rina was nothing more than a faded memory of a memory, a story I sometimes told. And those nine months were so joyful that she never crossed my mind. My pregnancy showed no signs of distress. I had the finest obstetrician available. We purchased special antique baby furniture. My husband, Brad, and I papered the baby's room in cabbage patch and bunny wallpaper. I made matching curtains—my first sewing project—and we laughed at the uneven slant of the hem. When I went into labor, I actually finished the last two chapters of the book I was reading before I called Brad at the office. I took a taxi and he met me at the hospital with a bouquet of daisies. We talked and laughed and cried and told stories until I reached my thirteenth hour of labor and it was clear all was not progressing smoothly. The pain grew and grew. I had planned on natural childbirth, but they convinced me to take a painkiller. While they administered it, my physician walked Brad out of the room. When they returned, they looked grim. Brad was frowning. Something was wrong, Brad said, very wrong. The doctor said they needed to do a C-section. Some of my friends had had C-sections and were fine, but all I could think of was Caesar—*rip open the mother to save the king!*

Brad held my hand as they wheeled me into another room. They located a vein inside my elbow to insert sodium Pentothal. The last thing I saw was the blur of Brad's face, next the flash and wink of a starched white uniform. Then I heard a woman's voice.

"Don't worry. Everything is going to be fine."

I thought it was a nurse, but when I opened my eyes, I saw Rina leaning over the stainless steel railing of my hospital bed, as clearly—*more clearly*—than I had seen Brad moments before.

"Really, Annie, the baby is going to be fine, plump and healthy, she's just in an awkward position, that's all. You're going to be fine too."

"Rina?" I asked. She was barefoot and dressed in a simple white shift. She smiled at me and stomped across the linoleum to a counter a few feet away. She boosted herself up, and sat, facing me, her feet dangling. Her hair was once again in a bouffant.

"Yeah, it's me. I'm a ghost or an angel—depending on how you want to look at it." Again she smiled.

"Where did you come from?"

"The moon," she said and laughed. "You're a really pretty woman, just like I knew you would be, but I see you don't keep your nails up."

She held her hands out for me to examine. Her nails were shell pink.

"Remember when we used to do yours?"

"How do you know everything will be fine?"

"Believe me, *I know,*" she said, plopping down from the counter. "I know those things. I was born with a web over my face. They had to peel it off. I have experience. I knew from the minute Daddy drove me up to the emergency room door that I wasn't going to make it but my son, Dominic—he was 'dopted out to an Italian family—was going to be fine. He's doing great. In fact, he lives just outside Chicago. I'm happy. Really I am. Ray is with me now; he went in a crash a year after me."

"Rina?" I said, trying to sit up, pull myself up with the bars of my hospital bed.

"Look, I've got to go. But I wanted to come special for you, to tell you it will be fine, you know, really good. I know your side of the family can be kinda high-strung. But don't worry. Your daughter will be beautiful."

Without even realizing I'd closed my eyes, I opened them once more. Brad was sitting beside me.

"We have a girl. A beautiful, healthy girl," he said. I closed my eyes and went to sleep.

Days later, when we were home and I was rocking our little girl in the antique rocker we'd purchased, I tried to tell Brad about Rina's visit. Brad was kind, not condescending, but he said the vision was undoubtedly drug or trauma induced. When I explained how real she was, he said it was natural that I would dream of Rina at a time like that. I found myself growing irritated with his disbelief, angry even; how then, I demanded, did I know in a dream that I was going to have a girl? Hurt by my sudden fury, he shrugged and said that there were only two genders to choose from, but if I really wanted to know I could probably investigate Indy car crashes that happened a year after Rina died, and maybe trace her child's adoption records. As suddenly as the anger welled inside me, it subsided. I knew I would never follow up. I didn't want to lose faith in what I had seen. I smiled at Brad, apologized for my temper, and leaned forward to whisper a lullaby in the pink shell of my daughter's ear.

Wrongs

Nine people stand in front of Adelaide in line. But since three postal workers are on duty, Adelaide counts herself as fourth. She figures it's the same thing since nine divided by three is three—three customers to each clerk. Good. She wants to get this over with quickly, get it out of her mind.

Adelaide looks at the carefully wrapped brown package in her hands. She tries to imagine Sara's face when she sees Adelaide's name in the return address corner. Will she sigh? Wince? Twist her face in that look she developed years ago—the strange mixture of sullenness, anger, and disinterest—and cram the package in the trash? No. Sara has always been a curious girl. She won't be able to resist opening a box addressed to her. Adelaide had to train Sara to be patient when opening gifts, not just rip into them like a starving animal. At her first birthday party where children her own age were invited, Sara was feverish with excitement over the multitude of packages. Adelaide remembers her round face, pale except for flushes on her cheeks, meshes of hundreds of fine, little scarlet scratches.

She was so different from her younger sisters, so defiant. Now everyone says it's genetics. *After all, Addy,* they say, *look at who her father was. She wasn't as lucky as the two younger girls to have Lewis as her natural daddy.* But when Sara was growing up, everything was attributed to environment, social psychology. *I treat all three of them the same,* Adelaide would plead. In response, friends and family shot her those annoyingly wise and patient smiles. Only her second husband, Lewis, seemed to have faith in genetics back then, in the early seventies. *It's in her blood,* he often said. *What did that mean,* Adelaide had asked, *that they should just give up?* No, it meant they needed to be a little stricter with Sara, a little less trusting. So, in fact, Sara's environment *had* been slightly different.

Shifting the package to cradle in one arm, Adelaide removes her glasses and rubs the bridge of her nose. She resisted getting glasses until she could no longer acquire her driver's license without them. Her vision had been bad for so long that now, with her glasses, she is often surprised by the sharpness of edges, the way things really look. But the frames cut into her nose, making slick little dents on each side. She frequently needs to remove them to massage her skin. This time it doesn't take long. Once she imagines the blood is circulating again, she pushes the glasses into place, shifts the package back into both hands, and looks around.

This postal branch is very modern, much more so than the one she usually goes to near her job. In fact, it's probably on the cutting edge of post offices. Cutting edge. A decorator's dream. She smiles at the thought of these funny expressions. But they're true. The glossy white walls are carefully lined with triangular art deco sconces shooting beams of light upward. Cathedral ceilings stretch to skylights buttressed by beams sporting recessed lights and enormous hanging ferns. The floor is laid in U.S. Postal–colored ceramic tiles: blue-gray, unadulterated primary red, white, and yellow. In the center is a lovely mosaic of the postal logo—the American eagle, his powerful wings drawn back in preparation for magnificent flight.

Behind the counter, the wall is decorated with everything they sell here—stamp collecting kits, rolls of mailing tape, teddy bears wearing sewn-to-fit postal uniforms, cardboard boxes, and padded envelopes in various sizes. Above the counter, a fancy electronic ticker tape—like the one in Times Square—rolls off friendly messages in cherry-red neon. "Have a Nice Day!" "We're Here to Serve You!" "Stamps Are a Good Investment!" "Fast Friendly Service!" Yet the faces of the three women seated beneath the ticker tape warn Adelaide not to be tricked by the surroundings. The place is not so hospitable as it may appear at first glance.

Though the first female clerk looks well past retirement age, she wears crimson lipstick and circles of rouge on her wrinkled white cheeks. Even at a distance of over six feet, Adelaide can see, with her new glasses, how deeper shades of red have collected in the woman's creases. Her cheeks remind Adelaide of sun-dried tomatoes. Paying her customer scant attention, the old woman shoots an endless stream of hushed talk at the coworker beside her. Adelaide strains to listen.

"He says he don't but I put a hair in my lock and it were disturbed when I come home. I know he's been in there. My stuffed animals are in a particular order and the rabbit was out of line yesterday. He thinks just cause he's the landlord he got a right to it, but he don't." She hands her customer a book of stamps without glancing up. "And I wouldn't be surprised if he got my phone tapped. I talked to my brother yesterday and two clicks come on the line out of nowhere and. . . ."

Her coworker, a middle-aged black woman, with beautiful mournful eyes and hair in tight sausage curls as if she had removed the curlers carefully to avoid disrupting the shapes, nods politely at everything the crazy old woman says. Yet the black woman's eyes remain only on her customer; she never turns to look at her older coworker.

"I could probably sue him for the whole building, the whole dang kit and caboodle, you know, for invasion of privacy. . . ."

The third postal worker is the strangest, a mass of ambiguities and contradictions. Huge and fat, nevertheless somehow vulnerable and beautiful. And powerful. She is young, probably not more than twenty-five. But her eyes are tired and hard. It is impossible to discern her race or ethnicity. She could be anyone's daughter—or everyone's. Her skin gleams a deep golden-raisin color. Her hair is a frightening shock of white-blond, neither curly nor straight. Her enormous eyes are sealed in ebony liner with tails curving outward from the lids, Cleopatra-style. And though she is the youngest of the three workers, presumably the one with least cause for bitterness, she is also, clearly, the angriest.

She hisses at a customer who has just arrived at her window. "Go back to your place, please."

"Huh?" asks the customer, a man in his sixties. "I'm next."

"I see that. But can *you* see the sign?" She lifts a beefy arm, cut into segments by the tight short sleeve of her light blue postal blouse and her biting watchband, and points to a sign on a pedestal at the head of the line:

WAIT HERE UNTIL CALLED

"You want me to go back to the line?"

"Nooow you catching on," she says, issuing a quick tight-lipped smile that is plainly no smile at all.

Cleopatra folds her arms on the counter and watches while the man walks back to the beginning of the line. As soon as he is once again at the front of the line, she calls out, "Next!"

"Me?" the man asks, his hand fluttering to his chest.

"Who else, mister, you next, right?" Cleopatra bellows, as if addressing the biggest idiot on the face of the earth. "And now you been called, ain't you?"

Three people still wait in front of Adelaide. She weighs her chances of getting Cleopatra. There is no way to know. It depends on how long each customer takes. She isn't in the mood to deal with Cleopatra. Adelaide wants to get this errand over with, put it behind her.

She looks at the package in her hands, the clear printing of Sara's new name, and thinks of the contents: Sara's dolls, a dozen of them, different shapes and sizes, the tallest a Barbie, the shortest a Girl Scout doll in uniform, some made of fabric, some hard plastic, others rubber, all facing the same direction. When Adelaide first placed the lid on the box she felt like she was closing the door on a packed elevator. Would Sara see them that way, a group of old friends arriving on a strange, free-flying elevator? Or would she see them as Adelaide intended: *Here, here is your childhood, the childhood you robbed yourself of, all packed neatly in a box*? What will she think? How will she interpret the unrequested arrival of her old playthings? Adelaide didn't include a note. What could she say that hadn't already been said a dozen times? Besides, how long had it been since Sara had listened to her?

Another skirmish is taking place between Cleopatra and a customer, a young businesswoman in a sharply tailored suit.

"Why won't you sell me one?" the woman demands.

"I told you, we all out," Cleopatra shrugs, her shoulders bristling with anger.

"But there's one right up there," the businesswoman insists, pointing—her left hand bears an engagement ring containing a diamond as big as a jelly bean—behind Cleopatra to where a ten-by-twelve-inch padded envelope hangs on the wall with a $1.25 price tag.

"That's on our display," says Cleopatra. "You can buy that same type envelope at the Jewel Grocery for just one dollar."

"I don't care about a quarter; I care about my time. That one is just hung up with a tack—couldn't you just take it down?"

The customer has pushed Cleopatra one step too far. Cleopatra crosses her arms on the counter, leans forward, and fixes her enormous eyes on the customer, her teeth clenched.

"Lady, *you* tryin' to tell *me* to dismantle a United States of America postal display?"

The businesswoman shakes her head angrily and stalks out of the office.

"Next!" calls Cleopatra merrily. Unstated, but strongly implied are the words *Who's next to be denied service?* Her attitude reminds Adelaide of Sara, twisting the rules to make a mockery of them. *Okay, you want me to go by the rules, well here I am playing by the rules, what's the matter now? You told me it was indecent to be living with a man almost twice my age, a car thief, okay so now we're married, no longer living together, what's the problem?* When, of course, being married to him only compounded the problem. *In America, I thought everyone was innocent until proven guilty. He wasn't convicted of anything, so what's the problem?* They all knew that he would have been convicted, along with Sara, if Lewis hadn't done some finagling with the victim's insurance company, if he and Adelaide hadn't used every spare dime they had to pay off the victim and get him to drop the charges. *Of course this is the thanks we get,* Lewis had said. *What do you expect? It's in her blood.*

Even now as Adelaide thinks of Sara and that man—*Sara's husband*—stealing the car, she is struck by the magnitude of such a crime, the raw nerve of climbing in something so big and solid as a car, someone else's car, and driving away, *just taking it.* In the old days, they shot horse thieves. Why not? What was worse than taking a person's power to move, to travel? A person's very freedom. It was only since Sara's crime that Adelaide realized the ease in which cars were stolen on television and the movies. Such a small crime in movies, yet life shattering when it's your daughter taking the car. *In her blood.* No, Sara's father had never stolen, at least not that Adelaide knew of, not objects, just luck; he had gambled, high stakes. But when his time had come, there had been no one to bail him out.

Adelaide is second in line now. The crazy worker's customer is having stacks of legal envelopes weighed. The black clerk beside her is filling out some kind of slip. Cleopatra is arguing with her customer.

"Sure, I tol' you, you can write a check. But you need three forms of I.D."

"No one requires three forms."

"This branch of the United States Postal Service of America requires three proper forms of I.D. to cash a check."

Adelaide remembers the obese bondsman, wearing a Hawaiian shirt, snakes of gold coiled around his neck, greasy skin, his fingers so wide that he could barely bring them together to clutch the phone, laughing when Adelaide showed him the balance in their checkbook. "With those kinda funds, you might as well begin lookin' for a new man. Itta be a better investment." Adelaide had been offended at the time; but in a way, hadn't he been prophetic? She had planned to wait the three years for Sara's father. She had told him she would always love him. But she had only visited him once, sitting primly on the other side of the Plexiglass and telling him about Sara's first steps, before filing for divorce.

It was almost a miracle that she had met Lewis, an insurance salesman with his own agency. He, in fact, became her insurance. He was neither handsome nor ugly, short nor tall. On workdays he wore short-sleeved shirts with broad striped ties, no sports coat, and on days off he donned golf shirts. *A straight shooter,* her father had said. A straight shooter who was devoted to making life easier for her.

Cleopatra's customer is flipping through all the compartments of his wallet. He pulls out a card to show Cleopatra.

"How about this?"

"A library card, mister, is not a proper form of identification for this facility, mister."

The man sighs and continues his search. *Take your time, mister,* thinks Adelaide, *at least until one of the other two clerks is available to wait on me.*

Studying Sara's new last name, Adelaide gently bounces her package in her hands. JoAnn, her youngest daughter, a junior in high school, the only one still at home, hadn't wanted Adelaide to mail it. *What are you doing with those?* she had asked when she had come across Adelaide piling the dolls into the box. *You can't get rid of those; Sara loved those; she called them her family.* It was true, Sara had loved her dolls. She had played for hours and hours alone in her room with them, had bathed them, had slept with them at night, had comforted them when they had had pretend illnesses. She had been careless and destructive with other toys, but kind and gentle to her dolls. Adelaide remembered how out of control Sara had always gotten when they played Monopoly together as a family. Sara would race the little steel dog around the board, making it bark wildly when she had to go to jail or pay a stiff rent. Lewis had always managed to remain calm when he reprimanded her: *Sara, if you don't want to act like a member of this family, you can go to your room.* It was Lewis who had said it, but Adelaide who had taken the brunt of Sara's anger. *It's you who doesn't want me in this family, you, you, you, you, you've got a new family, and you don't want me anymore!* The words had stung. After all, Adelaide probably wouldn't have married Lewis in the first place if she had not had Sara to care for. How could Sara have said such things? Lewis had always led her to her room patiently. *No, Sara, it's you. The other girls treat their mother with respect. That's why they get treated with respect in return, like members of the family.* Adelaide had wanted to talk to Lewis, tell him he was handling things wrong, but how could she when he did everything so patiently, so calmly? Instead, JoAnn had become Sara's defender. Sometimes she even followed Sara to her room and sat outside the door, in the hallway, talking softly to Sara throughout her confinement, despite the fact that Sara didn't respond.

"This isn't fair. I've got a driver's license and a major credit card," argues Cleopatra's customer.

Not fair; this isn't fair. Those were Sara's favorite words. *Not fair.* That's what JoAnn had said as well when Adelaide had told her she wasn't disposing of the dolls, just mailing them to Sara. *You're not being fair. She'll think we don't want her stuff here anymore, that we don't want her.*

"I don't make the rules, mister. Next!"

Adelaide looks around. The line has grown substantially behind her. No one stands in front of her. She is clearly next. Could she abdicate her turn? No. Undoubtedly she would be in trouble for violating procedure. She gathers her courage, straightens her shoulders, and walks toward the counter, her heels clicking hollowly against the tile floor. As she hands the package over to Cleopatra, Adelaide considers the power of modern communication in a way that makes her momentarily lose sight of Cleopatra's hostility. Adelaide thinks with amazement how the box that has just left her fingers will be accepted by Sara's in just a matter of days.

"I'd like to mail this first class, please," says Adelaide.

"Oh, you would, would you," retorts Cleopatra, snapping Adelaide out of her brief reverie. Cleopatra turns the package over to examine the seals, her brightly painted nails flashing blood red. "You see what type of tape is here, lady?"

Seldom in her life has Adelaide wanted to be right more than she does this second.

"Masking tape?" Adelaide asks, her voice almost a whisper. All the courage she felt walking to the counter evaporates.

"That's correct," says Cleopatra, her nonsmile spreading slowly across her face. Adelaide recognizes this as a bad sign. "And the United States Postal Service don't deliver nothing without proper mailing tape, do it?"

Adelaide summons all the strength she can. "I've mailed things with masking tape before."

"Not here you haven't."

"Oh, I think so," says Adelaide, simultaneously picturing a few boxes she mailed off last Christmas and wondering why she pushes her luck.

"Lady," says Cleopatra, "you wrong. Wro-NG. Wr-ONG. WRONG." Her voice grows louder with each "wrong." Her huge eyes are bulging. The irises are blue rimmed, deep brown in the center. Adelaide notices an intensity that wasn't present before, at the very moment she becomes aware of how silent the post office has fallen. All eyes— including those of the other two postal workers—are on her and Cleopatra.

"I know I've done this before," Adelaide says, her voice low and steady. But as the words issue from her mouth, Adelaide realizes with burning shame and fear that she used brown paper tape for those packages last year.

"Now, lady," says Cleopatra, her loud voice a frightening mix of pity, delight, and contempt. "Why you trying to make up excuses for yourself? You know you wrong." Her voice grows louder, booming even. This time she actually sings the words out. "You wrONG, WRONG, WRONGGGGG!" The last "G" rolls off her tongue as if she has reached the grand finale. Adelaide's face burns. She feels Cleopatra sees into her very soul, sees the many ways Adelaide has been wrong in the past, and continues to be wrong now. She sees how little Adelaide understands the world, the relationships that make up the world, the ubiquitous unfairness, the injustices, *the wrongs.* Didn't Adelaide fail to see who Cleopatra was beneath her uniform, her shocking white-blond hair, her flashing nails, her bulging eyes? Hadn't Adelaide failed her first husband, failed Sara? Failed to see that no matter how carefully she had stacked the dolls and wrapped the package, there was no way she could make wrong right?

"Oh," Adelaide mumbles. A few irreverent customers smile faintly, as if it's a great joke. The other customers, though staring, are clearly on Adelaide's side. They obviously think the affair is a simple matter of poor service. A few shake their heads and click their tongues. Adelaide doesn't acknowledge their support. She doesn't want to lend it validity. She is remembering Sara many years ago, the only dark-haired person in the family, accompanying her fair-haired sisters on report card day. She had been the last in the lineup to hand her card over. As she did, she collapsed in a puddle on the floor, sobbing. Adelaide and Lewis looked at the card at the same time. Amid the C's and B's only the D's stood out. *I can't do it,* Sara had cried. *Baby talk,* Lewis had retorted. *If you want to get all good grades, you can. Look at your sisters. This isn't a family of quitters.* Adelaide remembers how she had wanted to take Sara in her arms, hold her to her breasts, how she had restrained herself, feeling it would be wrong to undermine Lewis. Adelaide knows now how wrong she had been, why Sara had learned to distort the rules to survive in a world where what appears wrong is right, and what is right is really wrong. What choice did Sara have in a family where being rightfully unhappy, uncertain, made her an outsider? As Adelaide stands under the scrutiny of all those around her, her life seems like a conduit for propagating wrongs, series of wrongs, and, now, generations of wrongs: wrongs she had inflicted on Sara, her other girls, wrongs she had suffered gladly, and, saddest of all, wrongs she had refused to see at all.

The room remains hushed, waiting for Adelaide's reaction.

"Sorry," she says, clumsily seizing her package, and heading for the double doors. Her stride widens as she pushes the doors open with one extended arm, cuts across the anteroom, and shoves through more plate glass doors into the fresh air. On the curb, a deep-blue mailbox and a green-gray hooded trash can sit side by side, like a stooped couple that has been married for many long years. The two of them somehow seem to represent all the choices, all the options in the world. Adelaide hugs the package to her chest. She hopes that Sara has found some form of happiness with her new husband, or— given the unlikelihood of that in a world of such limited options— she hopes that Sara has at least experienced happiness, knows what it's like to be free from pain, even if only for the few days she had behind the wheel of the stolen car. Adelaide squeezes the package tighter, as if it's not too late to protect Sara, to go back in time and do it all over, and steps past the containers, off the curb.

Guests

"Really?"

—Oprah, *The Oprah Winfrey Show*

Derrick fished in the tight front pocket of his jeans for more change. He dug up two quarters and added them to the puddle of dimes in the bellboy's outstretched palm. When the bellboy didn't move, Derrick spoke.

"There's your gratuitous."

The bellboy snorted, a half-sigh half-sneer, and left the room, swinging the door shut behind him.

"What's his problem?" asked Amber. She possessed a suspicious nature. Actually, she was more than simply suspicious; she *knew* not to trust anyone, knew to just assume the worst.

"Who gives a shit. We get reimbursed," said Derrick. Then his eyebrows drew together in worry. "At least I think so; they said to save receipts."

"Hurry up, maybe you can catch him," said Amber, flinging her red plastic purse on the sofa, as if the gesture would whip Derrick into action.

Derrick took one uncertain step toward the door, then turned back to Amber.

"Aw, bellboys probably don't even give receipts. Besides, who gives a shit. Look, baby, look where we are. We've finally made it to the top!"

Amber started to protest. His last sentence irked her. She wasn't sure why. Maybe because it sounded fake, like deceitful bragging, man talk—whatever, it didn't sound real. "Finally" suggested a long struggle, and "made it" rang of permanence. But she bit her tongue. Amber knew she had a nasty tongue; lately she had really been working to control it. What with Rocky being almost two and all, it was silly to make trouble out of nothing. A few words. Besides, Derrick might not always catch on to people's motives, he might get cheated from time to time; but he was smarter with language than Amber—he always won out in arguments. Amber knew she wouldn't be able to express what she thought in words. So, she tried to relax and enjoy herself.

She surveyed the suite. The wall-to-wall carpeting was a luscious, thick lime green. In the section where they stood was a wet bar, a big screen television, and a sofa arrangement composed of a lime green and peach-colored pinstriped sofa and two Queen Anne's chairs upholstered in peach brocade. The arrangement circled a glass-topped coffee table holding a huge Chinese vase overflowing with flowers sprouting large peach blooms.

"Wow, everything is so, so, . . ." Amber tried to find the right word, *"clean."*

"I don't think we're in Kansas anymore, Toto." Derrick had heard that line about a year ago and taken a liking to it; *over-liking* was probably more accurate. This was at least the third time Amber had heard it today. When else had he said it? On the airplane when served the miniature bottle of vodka with his Bloody Mary (a drink he had never before ordered) and when the limo driver met them at the gate holding up the big cardboard sign that read "Derrick and Amber."

Hold your tongue, thought Amber.

Through open double doors at the far end of room was a king-size bed with a peach-colored spread. Amber strode toward it, her red leather boots snapping. She wanted to smooth her hand across the surface. It looked good enough to eat, like peach sherbet. The bed faced another television, but she couldn't stop to check it out. Beside the bed, the open door to the bath beckoned her. She walked straight inside.

"Oh my God, Derrick, come here, you've gotta see this!" She couldn't believe her eyes. Glass and mirrors and marble. The bathroom was as big as their living room at home. *Two* toilets. Three sinks. A walk-in shower. And right in the center, three steps led up to a round Jacuzzi, as wide as a wading pool but three times as deep. Derrick trotted up behind her.

"Holy shit," said Derrick over her shoulder. "Not Kansas, no sirree, not Kansas."

Amber wasn't even annoyed. She was too moved by the beauty of the bathroom to be bothered by anything.

"I wish it were mine," she said.

"It's just the start, babe, we're on our way now."

Well, almost nothing bothered her. This comment gave her the same sinking feeling she had had when he had said "we've finally made it." What bothered her? Not bragging. False hope? Amber's mama's favorite line used to be "now don't get your hopes up." All her life Amber had guarded against losing control of her hopes. And now, today, almost everything she did risked her one form of protection.

"I'm gonna take a bubble bath."

"Not now you're not." Derrick grabbed her upper right arm, firmly enough to imply a threat. "We're going out to dinner."

"Oh, Derrick, I don't wanna go out." She tried to say it as sweet as possible. She didn't want a fight tonight. Not tonight. Her face all red and puffy from crying. Tomorrow they'd be on television. The whole country was going to see her. Her entire family. Her best friend, Dee. All those jerks from her high school days. "Please, Derrick, we've got this beautiful place. It was a long ride from the airport. Let's stay here."

When he finally responded, his voice was measured. Each word left his lips like a tack being hammered into place.

"So we come all the way to fucking New York City and we don't leave the hotel." She could hear his anger mounting. "I get us on television. Fucking television. I get us our big break and you just want to sit inside."

Amber knew she needed to take desperate measures to save the situation. She hoped she wouldn't go too far. She couldn't let him know she was just trying to appease him.

"We could take the bubble bath together," she suggested, smiling. Invitingly. Hopefully. His grip slackened. She gently tugged her arm free.

"Whattaya say?" she asked in her sexiest voice.

A familiar two-second pause followed; it could go either way; he could see she was just buying time, call her a name, shove her against the hard marble floor—or he could go for it. His face softened.

He went for it!

"Run the water. I'll order us up some room service." He headed so fast for the bedside phone that his body slanted forward, his chin preceding his feet. Relieved, Amber let out a sigh and ran the bath. The faucet was a foot above the tub so that the water cascaded in a dazzling waterfall. She gasped at the sheer beauty of it, then sighed once more. Amber hated to screw in water. It felt rubbery. But she knew it really got men going. In high school, the guys had loved to do it in the school pool. And she knew if she could just tolerate it now, she would have the rest of the night to herself.

She only got a moment to soak before Derrick appeared in the doorway, triumphantly naked. He still had a good body. A bit of a beer belly, but athletic. It was the way he walked—like the grand conqueror, like the bath was his idea—that bugged her. He was erect. She smiled, almost laughed at the image of his thing growing and growing into a long serpent, popping out like one of those endless spring worms let loose from a fake peanut can. Her smile was genuine. She felt happy, happy that it would soon be over. She opened her arms in welcome. Soap bubbles clung to her wrists. Everything smelled of strawberry shampoo.

It was worse than she had expected. As Derrick pumped, jerking her up and down, soap stung her eyes. Water got in her mouth. Twice she slipped so deep beneath the surface that water surged up her nose, burning. She stood it only because she knew it couldn't take long. But after thrashing around for at least fifteen unbearable minutes, Derrick stunned her by withdrawing to let himself calm down. He had never done that before.

Once he was breathing evenly again, he pulled her slick body out onto the short stairway up to the Jacuzzi and mounted her so that she was pinned against the hard steps, their ledges pressed into her spine. The pain biting her back was so intense that she almost screamed, but just as she opened her mouth, she noticed his panting grow urgent. She waited until he shuddered and moaned, loud and long, and melted flat against her. She counted to ten before pushing at his shoulders, nudging him.

"Come on, get up, my back hurts."

Someone knocked on the door.

"Perfect timing," breathed Derrick, pushing himself up. He grabbed an enormous peach-colored towel from the rack, wrapped it around his waist, and padded from the room. Amber stood up—rubbing her throbbing back—dried herself, and wrapped her torso in a big towel. She had never felt such a lush towel, such softness. This, thought Amber, is what Rocky must feel like when I wrap him in a grown-up towel after a bath. Heaven. She tiptoed around the room exploring. There was a wonderful basket filled with miniature lotion bottles, fancy shampoos, soaps, and creams. Containers on the counter held Q-tips. And embedded in the wall mirror was a small magnifying mirror for applying makeup. She was intrigued by the way her skin looked in it, her pores as big as air holes on saltine crackers.

By the time she walked out, Derrick was sitting on the end of the bed, in his underpants, eating from a cart on wheels.

"What did you get us?"

"Surf and turf and champagne," he said, not looking up from the hunk of very red steak he was sawing with a knife and fork.

"Did you get mine well-done?" Amber hated anything rare. The sight of red juice made her a little queasy.

"Yeah, I know how you like it. But you should learn to appreciate meat cooked the right way. It might as well be hamburger when it's that burnt."

Gone was his anger of fifteen minutes earlier.

He clicked on the television facing the bed with the remote. They ate to the sound of their own chewing and canned laughter from a situation comedy neither of them had seen before.

"Hey, this is pretty good," said Derrick.

"The steak or the show?" asked Amber.

He looked at her and they both burst into laughter. They laughed and laughed. Derrick fell back on the bed. Amber grabbed her whole lobster from under the enormous silver bell covering her plate, leaned over Derrick, and danced the creature on its hind legs across Derrick's belly. Still laughing, Derrick sat up and pushed her down, ripping open her towel. She tried to squirm free, but was laughing too hard. Derrick pinned one of her shoulders to the bed. With his free hand, he seized the champagne bottle by the neck, and tilted it over her teasingly. Amber looked down at her expanse of stomach. Scarred with deep lines from her pregnancy, her stomach curved from her ribs to her hips like the face of a guitar. "No, no," she spat out between laughs. Derrick slanted the bottle more, trickling champagne into her belly button, then leaned forward to lap it out with his tongue. Amber laughed so hard that tears rolled down her temples to the bedspread. They laughed until they were spent, then Amber sat back up. It felt like old times. Finally, everything was going well. The trip felt right to her. She ate her meal heartily, even licked the excess lobster butter from her plate.

"You know," said Derrick, pulling on his jeans when his plate was clean. "I think I'm gonna go out, get me a beer in the hotel bar, and check out the action there. Do you wanna come?"

His anger had completed disappeared. Amber knew she wouldn't suffer a penalty for refusing. Some people might not recognize the logic of his anger, his needs, but Amber did. That was one of the reasons she stayed with him. She understood him and he understood her. Even when it was wrong or didn't make sense.

"No, I think I'll just hang out in the room, finish the bath. I want to look rested for tomorrow."

"Okay, well I won't be long."

She believed him. He was alone in New York; no friends around to goad him, coax him into staying out until all hours.

Alone, Amber added more hot water to the bath, climbed in, and soaked for a good half hour. She wished the kids she knew in high school could see her now. In a luxury bath in a fancy New York hotel. She tried to recall some of their faces, then was sorry she did. She winced at the thought of the football players lined up by the cafeteria at lunchtime, taunting her. "Hey Am-butt, hear you had a good time the other day. Wanna meet me in the locker room after the game tonight?" She squeezed her eyes tight to erase the memory. She knew it was dangerous to even think about them. If Derrick knew the stuff she had done with them, he might kill her. It was better not to even let them enter her mind—less danger of her mentioning them.

Instead she concentrated on Rocky, imagined him asleep in his Porta Crib at Derrick's mother's house. She hoped Derrick's mother wasn't pushing him too hard on the toilet training. She knew Derrick's mom was bugged that Rocky wasn't trained yet; she claimed Derrick was trained when he was nine months, wouldn't pee unless she took off his diapers and held him above the toilet. Amber didn't believe her, but she knew better than to mess with Derrick's mom. Amber closed her eyes.

She soaked for another half hour, used a brand new towel to dry herself off, put on the negligee she had purchased just for the trip, and slid beneath the sheets of the gigantic bed. The bed was made so tightly that she felt like she was pressed between the pages of a book. She clicked on the television. Only talk shows. Watching them made her think of her guest appearance the next day, which made her nervous. So she clicked the mute button and picked up the phone. She dialed Dee's number at home in Oklahoma.

"Dee?"

"Oh my God, Amber, are you calling from New York City?" She heard Dee cup the phone and call out to someone else, probably Dee's mother, in a muffled voice, *It's Amber, calling me all the way from New York.* "I can't believe you called!"

"Dee, you just wouldn't believe this place," said Amber. She searched for the words to describe the airplane ride, the limo, the suite, the bathroom, but she couldn't think of any so she just gave up. "What are you doing?"

"Watching TV."

"Me, too. What are you watching?" They turned to the same station and discussed the dresses of the women. Then they watched together silently for a while the way they often did on the phone at home. "Well, I guess I better go. Long distance and all."

"Break a leg!" said Dee.

Amber woke up a full two hours before the limo was due. She was as nervous as she had been on the first day of kindergarten. After that, she never really cared about school again—but she always remembered that first day with longing, the new plaid jumper laid out on her bed, the two saddle shoes waiting so hopefully at the foot of the bed. Her mama had been proud to buy her three brand-new outfits for school. But the first day had been a disaster; Amber had come home crying. She didn't remember what went wrong, only the doubtful look in her mama's eyes when she told Amber, "Don't worry, it will get better." Of course, it hadn't. Amber tried to push her mama from her thoughts; she didn't like to think about her. The memory of her mama always made her sad.

Derrick was still asleep on his side of the bed, so Amber laid out her clothes on the other side. The producer had told her not to wear black or white, so she had purchased a really pretty pale blue mohair sweater with pink and red rhinestones sprinkled across the yoke and shoulders like angelic dandruff. She had also bought a new pair of stonewashed jeans (the producer had said to dress casual) and the red leather boots (real leather uppers—they set off the red in the rhinestones and her purse). For weeks, she had imagined how she would look on the panel: her knees crossed, showing off her red boots, red sparkles amid the pale cloud of blue on top. Perfect with her light blond hair and fair skin.

She placed the red boots at the foot of the bed and went in the bath to wash her hair and do her makeup. The producer had said they could "apply it" at the station, but "most guests preferred just to do their own makeup." The way the producer had phrased it, Amber knew they preferred she do it herself. Amber didn't care; she didn't trust them to do it right; besides, something bothered her about the snotty way the producer had said *apply.*

Amber washed her hair in the walk-in shower and blew it dry in front of the mirrored wall over the sinks. She couldn't help but smile at the results. Her new cut looked great. Really stylish—feathered on the top, just like she had short hair, but real long in the back. Fascinated with the effect, she turned from side to side. She loved the way her hair hung straight down her back between her shoulder blades without being any fuss on the sides or top, like a veil held in place by a crown.

Then she peered in the magnifying mirror. It was perfect for doing makeup. (Fuck *The Judy True Show* producer!) Right under her brows, Amber applied a band of white, then a band of very pale blue— an exact match to her sweater—then the eyeliner, thick black on top, dark brown on bottom. The rest was easy: two streaks of brick-colored blush on each cheek and pink lipstick.

After she woke Derrick up, she sat perfectly still on the brocade sofa waiting for him to shower and shave. She didn't want to mess herself up.

In the back of the limo, she grew nervous again.

"Derrick, what if I screw everything up? Say something dumb?" He took her hand. "Should we rehearse or anything?"

"No, it'll sound bogus if we rehearse; it's better to have a natural presentation. Just use a little more formal words than you do every day."

"Shit, Derrick, I'm scared." She could feel panic closing her throat. "What do you mean formal words?"

"Don't worry. I'll do most of the talking." He squeezed her hand gently for reassurance. This really scared her. If he was merely anxious, he would take his frustration out on her. He must be scared witless to be so nice. For the rest of the ride to the studio, they were both silent.

Everyone—there must have been a million assistants—fussed over them at the station, saying how great they looked, how terrific the show would be, how fortunate they were to be chosen. Amber could see Derrick getting reinflated with the compliments, his chest actually puffing up. But she sank lower; she knew these people didn't give a shit about her; no one ever had. But for Derrick's sake, she smiled and nodded her head at all the instructions—to remove her chewing gum, not to pay attention to Judy True's cue cards, or to worry about the camera, just look straight ahead, not to use last names, keep their chins up.

Fifteen minutes before the audience was to fill the studio, they were introduced to Judy True (who looked much older in real life, her eyes blue stones pressed into the thick pancake makeup and her hair stiff with spray) and the other guests on the panel—a very fat couple (the woman, Amber noted, wore black despite the producer's directions) and an older hippie-type couple. Then assistants took them all out onstage to get used to it, feel comfortable, without the pressure of an audience. Amber had rarely experienced such a sense of unreality as she did on that stage. The towering ceilings. Pots of fake flowers. The bright lights. The thin mock walls of the set. Many smiling faces. Everyone treating her so special. Everything artificial. It was as unreal as her mother's funeral, the drugs and bright lights of the hospital for Rocky's birth. The assistants led them back off the stage to the greenroom. "Just like on *The Tonight Show*, babe," Derrick whispered to her. Amber could get no comfort from him. He was as high as she'd ever seen him.

Even time had no reality. They were escorted to the greenroom an hour before airtime. She blinked her eyes and it was ten minutes until air. Time for individual last minute pep talks, fastening the tiny microphones.

Amber felt nauseated. Heidi, the girl adjusting Amber's mike, looked extremely young, younger than Amber. Not very glamorous. Plain clothing and a simple haircut. Amber stared at the halo shining on the crown of Heidi's hair as she bent to affix Amber's mike beside a red rhinestone. Could Amber trust her? Could Heidi help her? Get her out of this?

"I don't know if I should do this," said Amber, her voice a thin whisper. "I think I'll be embarrassed, you know, talking about sex on television."

Heidi looked up into Amber's face and smiled, teeth as big and bright white as new piano keys.

"There's no reason to be embarrassed. You're helping other people by sharing your problems," said Heidi. "You're going to be terrrrrific!"

Heidi stared right at her, but Amber had a feeling Heidi didn't see her. Had Amber been so absorbed by this whole new unreality that she ceased to exist? She watched the other guests being led off to the stage.

"I don't . . ." started Amber.

"Now, don't be selfish!" said Heidi, still smiling, managing to look both upbeat and disappointed at the same time. "Show some courage. Think of all the people you'll be helping."

Heidi took her hand. Amber had never held hands with another woman before—it felt funny, the soft little fingers—but she rather liked it. Heidi led her out to her seat beside Derrick in the row of chairs onstage. The fat couple was at one end. She and Derrick at the other. The hippies in the middle. Judy True stood just offstage in the center aisle. The room was packed.

"Ten seconds!" someone shouted. " . . . three, two, one."

The lights became brighter.

"Welcome to *The Judy True Show*!" said Judy, talking into her hand mike, staring just to the left of Derrick at her cue cards. "We've got a great show for you today. Couples who—you aren't going to believe this!—actually went without sex for a year or more, while sleeping side by side *in the same bed*. But now, here's the best part—all three of the couples on our panel today have corrected their problems and are making whoopee even *better than before*! Today, they will share their secrets for great sex.

"First we have Cathy and Bill, who, until they lost fifty pounds each, were actually too fat to get it on. [Laughter from the audience, smiles from Cathy and Bill.] Next, in the center, we have Jeff and

Meredith who used to have trust issues. [Groans of disapproval from the audience, deadpan stares from Jeff and Meredith.] And last, we have a couple who I'm sure a lot of you can relate to, Derrick and Amber, who lost the desire after Amber had a difficult first pregnancy. [Sighs of sympathy, a big grin from Derrick.] Well, Derrick," continued Judy True, ad-libbing. "You look like a happy man. I can see from that Cheshire-cat grin that things have changed." (Lots of laughter.)

"They sure have, Judy," said Derrick.

"Why not tell us when you first noticed a problem."

"Well, of course, I anticipated a period of sexual postponement after the genesis of our son, but I first experienced a issue around two months following the commencement of the birth. When my wife, Amber Lynne, was still residing in the hospital facility, our physician informed us to anticipate a period of sexlessness for about approximately one month. When that era of time had concluded, I detected some concern."

Amber had no idea what Derrick had just said. She thought maybe he was laying the formal language on too thick. But he sure sounded smart.

Judy True dismissed him with one quick sweep of her eyelids, before turning her attention to the first couple.

"Bill and Cathy, can you share with the audience how long the two of you went without sex?"

"Five years," said Bill. (Gasps from the audience.)

"Well, intercourse, that is," said Cathy. "We fooled around. We just couldn't do it. Bill weighed nearly three hundred and I weighed two eighty. And, by the way, *Bill* lost fifty pounds, *I* lost ninety-five!"

A big smile from Judy True.

"Good for you, Cathy. Let's hear it for Cathy, folks." (Loud applause from the audience.) "How did you do it, Cathy?"

"One day at a time." (More applause.)

"Okay, now, what about you two, Jeff and Meredith?"

"We used to be really, you know, hot for each other," said Meredith. "But then we decided to go, you know, open—have an open marriage, pursue other pleasures so to speak. At first it was great. Then Jeff got jealous."

"It was a trust issue," said Jeff. "I didn't trust her anymore. It was ironic since the whole open business started as an honesty thing, but I started imagining her with other men. I didn't believe her even if she said she was at the grocery store."

Amber could feel Derrick getting antsy beside her. He wanted another chance to speak.

Judy True looked concerned.

"Jeff, did anything happen to make you distrust Meredith?"

"Well, yeah," he said, giving Meredith a sideways glance. "She said she slept with this one friend of ours just once, but it turned out to be a regular thing." (Gasps from the audience.)

"That's not true!" shouted Meredith. "I never said 'once.'"

"Well, you implied it."

"I did not."

"Did too."

"Hold on, you two," said Judy True. "I see lots of hands from the audience." Judy strode over to the second row, stretching her mike between three people. An older woman with thick glasses stood up. She leaned toward the mike, her glasses slipping down the bridge of her nose.

"I was just wondering," said the woman, pushing her glasses back up with her thumb, "if anyone on the panel has ever sought counseling for these issues?" (The audience coos in approval.)

Judy True nodded. "Good question. And we'll be back with the answer to that question and plenty more after this short commercial break."

The lights dimmed. Assistants ran everywhere. Some out into the audience. Others up to talk to the guests. Only Judy True remained still, her arm down, the mike resting beside her hip. She looked like a windup doll turned off for the commercial. Assistants buzzed around her, reapplying her makeup, puffing up her hair.

A young male assistant leaned into Derrick's face.

"Ah, Derrick, buddy," the assistant touched Derrick's shoulder warmly, "could you try and speak more casually?"

Derrick looked crestfallen.

The assistant winked. "Not everyone out in television land is a brain trust. You need to speak down to their level."

Derrick smiled, relieved.

"Gotcha, buddy," he said.

The lights flashed brighter.

"Ten seconds to air. Okay . . . three, two, one."

Magically, Judy True came back to life.

"If you just tuned in, we're talking to couples who abstained from sexual relations for a year or more. A member of our audience just asked if any of our guests has undergone counseling. Cathy, I'll start with you."

"I'm not sure, does Weight Watchers and Overeaters Anonymous count?" (A few chuckles from the audience.)

"Come on, people," chided Judy True, twisting her neck to rake her eyes over the audience. "You're not being fair. Cathy asked a serious question and we owe her a serious answer." (Scattered applause.) Judy turned back to Cathy triumphantly, a queen pronouncing knighthood. "Yes, Cathy, I believe it *does* count. Any help you receive from an institution outside your immediate family constitutes taking that first step." (Applause.)

"Judy," said Derrick, "I'd like an opportunity to respond to that question. I didn't think we had to utilize counseling because time would adjust our situation." (Applause.)

Amber wasn't sure why everyone clapped. Had Derrick said something particularly revealing or insightful?

"Why didn't you resume sexual relations once Amber recovered? Did you find her less attractive after childbirth?"

"No, Judy, it wasn't the Madonna/whore thing—I saw your program on that—it was that Amber wasn't turned on. I utilized every means I had, but Amber was like a dead fish."

In her head, Amber pictured Derrick using all sorts of machinery on her limp body. It wasn't true. He didn't try anything. In fact it had been less than a year after Rocky's birth before they had sex, more like six months, but Derrick said that was close enough when he saw the show advertisement for guests. She remembered his exact words, *We might as well at least get a fucking trip to NYC out of this.* It was after a producer called to say they were accepted that he began getting grander ideas, thinking of their appearance as more than a free vacation.

"Amber?" Judy True said like she had said it more than once. Realizing she must have spaced out, Amber twitched. How could she have spaced out on national television?

"Huh?"

"You've been pretty quiet so far. Why don't you tell us why you weren't interested."

"It didn't feel right." Where did those words come from?

"How? Was it still painful from your delivery?"

"No. It didn't feel like anything. I mean I didn't feel anything. I can't put it into words."

"And now?"

"You should have seen us in the Jacuzzi at the hotel last night," interrupted Derrick. (Wild laughter from the audience.)

The sound of the audience laughter was almost deafening. Amber couldn't even hear what Derrick was saying, but the audience loved it. She tried to pay attention, but felt herself drifting off from the panel. She caught just a line of a story from the fat couple. *Feeling like two beach balls trying to mate.* (Raucous laughter.) Bits and pieces of the hippie couple arguing like they were in divorce court and the audience was the jury. *That wasn't our agreement,* said the man. (Encouraging jeers from the audience.) Amber didn't even *want* to hear; she needed to figure out how to put what she meant into words if she was called upon again. In school she had hated to be called on. She had always sat in the back, never raised her hand. She had never been capable of forming sentences out of what she knew, how she felt. Now, here she was on national television. She wondered if any of her old teachers would watch when it aired in Oklahoma. Any of her high school classmates. The boys on the football team. Then she realized that's what it meant to *feel.* The boys on the team, being so sweet to her, petting her hair, rubbing her shoulders—so sore from waitressing after school—stroking her breasts with such awe, like her breasts were special, *she was special,* whispering in her ear, persuading her, gently coaxing her behind the bleachers, the backseat of someone's car, the school pool after hours. Everything was fine until the time Randy Boucher got her into the boys' locker room with Charlie Trand and Mark Wollicome right outside the door in the hall. Randy was all gentle at first. Then after they did it on the locker room bench, Amber still prostrate on the bench, her butt pressed against it, a leg loped over either side so she was bent back from the knees like she was dancing the limbo, Randy jumped up. He went out in the hall and called "Next!" like they were at McDonald's. Charlie came in, laughed, squeezed both her nipples really hard, walked back out, and called "Next!" just like Randy. Then Mark came in, undid his pants, screwed her without saying "hi" or even pulling his jeans down. The stiff fabric and open zipper scraped her thighs. He zipped back up, then left, never uttering a word.

Nothing was the same after that.

Those boys took something from her and she couldn't get it back. She couldn't even figure out what they took or how they managed to keep it. From just that one time, how could they have a part of her forever? She was lost until she met Derrick. He and his mom had come to Oklahoma to work for his second cousin a year after Amber graduated high school. The fact that Derrick was less gentle, more matter-of-fact about sex than the other boys made Amber trust him; since her body didn't feel all loose, without joints, when she and Derrick screwed, she felt in better control. Then, after Rocky came, it was different, like she didn't even exist. Derrick was so matter-of-fact that he didn't see her. Only her body.

But she couldn't say any of that on television.

She saw it didn't matter. The fight between the hippie couple was consuming the show. Then Derrick was talking again, about the importance of foreplay. Then the beach ball couple, about feeling good about your body, the hippie couple about passion and control. Then the show ended. They were led offstage.

"Can you believe those two hogging so much of the show?" Derrick whispered in her ear. "But, hey! I got in some good ones, didn't I, babe? They really liked the stuff about the Jacuzzi. I wonder if any of the bigger programs, *Donahue* or *Oprah*, will be doing a show on this topic."

In the greenroom, Amber stayed away from Derrick and the other guests all congratulating each other on their performances while they waited to see the tape. Amber stood next to the door, which was opened just a crack. The audience streamed past on their way to the exit. Amber caught snippets of conversations. She strained to hear, wondering if anyone would mention her clothing or hair.

"That fat guy, what's his name, I think he was an enabler; he wants to keep her fat, if. . . ."

"Meredith would be better off without that. . . ."

"Where do they find all those lowlifes?"

Amber felt stung. She discreetly pushed the door shut and joined the others. Immediately the door opened again. Heidi stuck her head inside. "Watch the screen. Your show will be on in a minute."

The beach balls each took a chair, and Amber and Derrick shared the couch with the hippie couple. They all stared up at the television affixed to the ceiling. The *Judy True* logo appeared on the blank screen, then Judy herself, looking ten years younger than she had looked just moments earlier.

"Welcome to *The Judy True Show*! We've got a great. . . ."

Transfixed, Amber watched the show unfold on screen as if she were watching a magic box that had captured all their spirits. She had seen herself in Derrick's mom's home videos. But this was different. It was like she was here and there both at once. In the greenroom and on television. No, she thought, looking at her fancy red boots, her pale blue sweater, her wonderful haircut, it was like she was *just* up on screen. She wasn't in the greenroom at all.

Derrick nudged her and whispered, "Here it comes, baby. The part where you talk."

She saw the camera zoom in on her face, almost as close as in the magnifying mirror. Her hair looked short—the long part wasn't visible from the front. Her perfect eye makeup, three bands of color, arched above her eyes in a rainbow of white, powder blue, and black. Amber watched herself blink, preparing to speak. She had no control over the person on the screen. She couldn't stop her, couldn't prevent the woman in the box from giving away any more of herself. Amber had no power to shape or influence the words as they left her mouth. The pink lips moved, " . . . I mean I didn't feel anything. I can't put it into words."

Burying the Dead

eographically, Ohio isn't so terribly far away. Yet, for me, Ohio is a distant land, the place of my childhood: shimmering fields of mustard seed, of rusty trailer parks, developments crisscrossed with streets of 1950s starter homes, playing outdoors until the streetlights flickered on, catching fireflies, collecting polished buckeyes, of sleepy little towns like ours with starched white houses, and—most of all—of rich Ohio earth, perfect for shaping mud patties (deep brown and pliable), growing corn and wildflowers, and for burying the dead in shady hillside cemeteries.

So as I drive up Mill Road, past fields of weeds and Queen Anne's lace, the sewage treatment plant, the Shell station heralded by the huge glowing saffron-colored half shell atop a pole, it's no wonder I imagine that all the old trees, gas pumps, and fence posts rise from the earth like spirits as I approach. I cannot fathom they existed all this time without me. Like me, they must be returning for the funeral, called forth to revisit a distant land. Rounding the corner into town, I imagine all the familiar landmarks following me; ghostly, vaporish skins cast by their former structures, forming a parade behind me up Mill Road. *We're back! We're back!* I veer onto Dressler Street, then straight down to Main, the village green, the row of shops I visited with my mother when I was a girl so she could talk with her friends who were clerks, the soda fountain—*still there!*—where we all hung out as teenagers. As I approach Barberry Lane, my heart races, actually spins, as if on a rotisserie. I take the turn. The row of familiar white houses springs from the earth. My parents' house is among them, third on the left. The old oak is still in the front; for the first time in years I envision the place where the ridges in the bark separate, to bypass a knot, meeting on the other side. How many times did I look at that image and wonder what it meant? What it represented? (For certainly it was a secret sign.) I see the stump that once held the elm, felled—to the distress and tears of my mother—after the summer of Dutch elm disease. Cars crowd the driveway.

Pulling up to the curb, I notice the paint on the shutters and front door is chipped and peeling. Last time I was here it looked fresh. I feel the house is falling apart before my eyes. How could it age and decay without me? A woman crosses the drive, carrying a Corningware casserole, an aluminum foil cover rising like a tin mountain from the rims, glinting in the late afternoon sun. Two younger women accompany her; they resemble each other. Both have faded red hair, as if the color had come out in the wash. Yes, of course— my heart stops spinning—Mrs. McIhenny and the McIhenny twins. The recognition calls forth a memory, long suppressed, forgotten. Before me now like it never left: my first funeral, one that would have never taken place without me. I wonder, would I ever have remembered if I hadn't driven up, just now, for my mother's funeral just as Mrs. McIhenny and her daughters marched up the driveway? Or would that memory have remained buried, lost to me forever?

The story of that funeral starts with a fat girl, Debbie Driscoll, and her beautiful mother, Helena Driscoll.

Debbie was always anxious to be popular, even in fourth grade before the popular cliques had formed. Maybe her mother's stunning looks constituted a type of prophecy. Being confronted continually with such glamour must have been hard for a little fat girl. So she always planned events to win people over.

For her twelfth birthday, Debbie and her mother took me and Leslie Landham (a girl with cotton candy–blond hair who would eventually be voted homecoming queen) to a special restaurant on the top floor of Higbee's Department Store in Cleveland. On the hour-and-a-half drive from our little town into Cleveland, Debbie stood on her knees in the front seat, her back turned to the windshield so she could face Leslie and me. She wore a navy sweater, navy kneesocks, and a navy and red kilt with a huge brass safety pin holding the flap in place. Leslie and I wore party dresses. Debbie's hair was cut in a pageboy, her bangs slanting as straight as an edge of loose paper across the middle of her brow. I remember the flush of her cheeks as she spoke, her chubby fingers hooked over the backseat. *"Just wait until you see.* You've never seen a meal served like this. Have they, Mom? *Just wait.* You won't believe it."

Helena Driscoll kept her eyes on the road and didn't answer. I watched Debbie's lips. I had a visceral reaction to the way her upper gums showed when she spoke; but I knew such feelings were superficial so I fought them off and forced myself to look directly at her gums and smile.

At the restaurant, the maître d' escorted us in a winding path between tables. Helena Driscoll's silk dress rustled as she walked. In the center of each table, a miniature lamp with a tiny fluted cupcake-wrapping shade cast a yellow pool of light. At a table overlooking the blinking lights of Cleveland proper, our guide pulled out a chair for Mrs. Driscoll. She shot the man a closed-lip salmon-pink smile. At that moment, I realized that the main reason I liked to play at Debbie's house on Skytop Lane—rather than at my own— was her mother. In the same way her presence must have taunted Debbie with visions of a bleak future, Helena Driscoll provided me with material for envisioning a glamorous future. For at the time, I believed my womanhood would be a series of expensive nightclubs (like the one where Ricky Ricardo performed), exclusive parties, and glittering gowns. It didn't matter that Helena Driscoll seemed no more interested in me than my own mother; there seemed a chance with her. She was so alone, such a romantic figure, that I imagined there was room for me. I thought that in another life we could be friends, confidantes even. The glamour of the restaurant and the view seemed a hint of what was to come.

Mrs. Driscoll crossed her legs, opened the huge menu—as big as a child's picture book—and lit a cigarette.

"Order us what I had last time," said Debbie.

Without a word, Mrs. Driscoll closed the menu and placed it back on the table. She looked bored. Her bright salmon lips slipped into a pout, her eyes stared over our heads, out the window. She pulled a sleek black holder from her purse and inserted her smoking cigarette. This gesture transported me to heaven. Debbie was not so moved. It was *her* party and she wanted her mother's attention, her assistance in establishing Debbie's hostess prowess.

When the meal was served, Debbie's promises, at first, seemed fulfilled. A grand presentation. The way I remember it—though my recollection seems absurd given we were in Cleveland in the early sixties—three waiters, one behind the other, sashayed across the dining room weaving between tables, supporting silver trays high above their heads on the fingertips of their white-gloved hands. Each tray featured a white cardboard oven suitable in size for a squirrel standing on his hind legs to fry sparrow eggs. With simultaneous flourishes, the individual ovens were placed in front of Debbie, Leslie, and me: perfect replicas of modern 1960s ovens. Each was constructed of thick and sturdy cardboard. Along a panel at the back of the oven top were knobs and temperature gauges stamped in black. On the stove surface, printed black burners held miniature saucepans: one with peas, one with cooked carrots, and one with mashed potatoes. I pulled open my cardboard oven door. Inside sat a tinfoil roaster, like a single square lifted from a TV dinner, brimming with three thin turkey slices and congealed gravy.

When we took our first bites, the magnificence of the presentation was eclipsed by the reality of the meal. The feast was sad: the portions tiny (the saucepans yielded no more than two large spoonfuls each) and the quality a notch below the school cafeteria hot lunches. I could barely swallow the mealy yellow-green peas. And on top of this, we were simply too old. The meal was conspicuously babyish.

Helena Driscoll nibbled on shrimp salad without extinguishing her cigarette. Instead, she turned her chair out from the table, so she could smoke between small bites. Despite her obvious indifference to us, I was impressed. I admired her high cheekbones, the manner in which her wavy hair brushed her shoulders, and I simply loved the way she smoked her cigarette—as if the very act of inhaling, each long drag, carried her further away from us three girls. To a land I would someday travel.

Surprisingly the food's quality didn't slow us down. We were greedy little girls. We finished what was edible of our meals in minutes. Leslie actually licked clean one of her saucepans, her pink tongue quickly swiping the edges. When she placed the pan back on a burner, Mrs. Driscoll came out of her dreamworld. She looked at our clean saucepans, our empty ovens, and crushed her cigarette out in the sparkling crystal ashtray. The white filter was ringed with salmon lipstick.

"In another year, you girls will be too old for this," she said. I marveled at the social skill her remark revealed. In one unapologetic line, she managed to acknowledge both the lilliputian portions and the childish concept without accepting blame. Her statement clearly implied the mistake was not *hers*. She had planned well. *Technically* we were still young enough; we were simply one year ahead of our time. Debbie, however, completely missed her mother's adroitness; she couldn't drop the matter.

"Mother," she whined, as only a fat girl could. "They used to have more food in these ovens, didn't they?"

Debbie's eyes pleaded with her mother. I winced. I knew Helena Driscoll wasn't going to wink at Debbie and say, *Oh, you're sooo right, Debbie, now I remember; they used to be much bigger, more luscious meals.*

"No, they're the same size. You're just getting older, Debbie. They seemed larger when you were younger."

This was the worst thing she could have said; not only had she failed to fall in with Debbie, but she had also suggested that both Debbie's judgment and her memory were off. Still, Debbie couldn't let well enough alone. Her desperation was a pitiful thing to witness. You could actually see her thinking, groping for ways to save her credibility. At last she remembered something that she hoped would redeem the situation.

"The ovens!" she cried, brandishing hers above her head like a trophy, her eyes wild and anxious. "You can keep them! We have to return the pots and pans, but we can take the ovens home. They're ours, all ours!"

She stared ahead at nothing, her lips parted to reveal her gums. Such a pathetic victory forced me to look away. Debbie was a broken girl.

I saw little of Debbie after that. She never called. We stopped making the trek between her house on Skytop and mine on Barberry. I knew I should make the first move, but I hadn't yet acquired the necessary tact to dismiss the inadequacy of the meal gracefully. Besides, I sensed the subject was taboo. How could I propose that anything as seemingly inconsequential as mashed potatoes, peas, turkey, and cardboard ovens had placed this strain on us? No, it could not be stated aloud. Never admitted. Yet the tension was palatable. For years, Debbie and I avoided each other. If I was thirsty in the school hall and Debbie was in line at the drinking fountain,

I would go stick my head under the faucet in the girls' bathroom to quench myself. If the only empty locker in gym class was next to mine, she simply left her clothing in a heap on the floor. Not until high school, when her mother ran off with another man, did we begin speaking again. She lost weight, a feat that resulted in revealing attractive features—her gummy smile even acquired a certain charm—but otherwise she was a mess. Frequently drunk or stoned, she had fallen from a straight-A student to a druggie. Her bouncy pageboy now a stringy tangle, her once clear skin oily and gray. Foolish as it may sound now, I never attributed Debbie's decline to her mother's abandonment, but rather assumed it was a natural outcome of the birthday fiasco. Who wouldn't need to anesthetize oneself against such a painful memory?

But immediately following the party—regardless of our lack of contact—I felt a staunch loyalty to Debbie. Perhaps I was atoning for my guilt at using her to be near her mother? Whatever, this loyalty found form in the oven. I couldn't bring myself to throw it away. My heart actually ached to think of the oven in the trash, soiled with coffee grounds and cigarette ashes. As if Debbie, herself, had been cruelly discarded. So I strove to make use of the mock appliance.

Most often, the oven functioned as a prop. Pretending to be a theater director, I would sit in the center of my pink fluffy bedroom rug with the oven surrounded by my Ginny dolls who served as the actors. Most of my friends had Barbies, svelte single-women dolls with doll boyfriends and doll cars. But I preferred Ginnies. They were chubby little prepuberty girl dolls, five inches tall with bendable elbows and knees. Though I knew I should be outgrowing them, I loved them so much that I didn't want to give them up. I adored the way the dolls' knees and elbows moved, snapping in and out of place like real-life prostheses. I revered the delicate little fingers and nails etched on their tiny hands, the blue glass eyes that opened and closed, the banks of thick black lashes that blinked up and down, the little-girl swells of their molded plastic bellies. And I particularly loved my favorite Ginny, a flaxen-haired beauty whom I called Bonita.

Bonita was the first Ginny I ever owned, and it showed. From the way the thin sealer on her face flaked she looked like she was in the final stages of sunburn or suffering from a curious disease. And she was balding. In order to make her walk, I pinched the crown of her acorn-sized head between my fingers. The hair on the spots I held tightest—right above her ears—was coming unglued. I could still manage to plait one pipe cleaner–sized braid down her back (using the rubber band from my brother Tim's retainer), but it looked like a strange mohawk or a snake dangling from her skull.

Since Bonita was my favorite, I always made her the star (after the oven, that is) of my miniproductions. The shows were silly or formulaic: copies of television shows or my own pointless, meandering plots. But, of course, my task was enormous considering all I had to work with was a balding doll and a cardboard oven too large for her.

In my biggest extravaganza, Bonita led a band of Ginnies on a complicated route from Tim's room, along the hall baseboards, through the bathroom, around the dangerous rim of the toilet bowl, back along the baseboard, into my room, through the dust balls swirling like doll tumbleweeds under my bed, across the fluffy pink rug to discover hidden treasure—my mother's pearl necklace—inside the oven.

Yet in the end, my attempts to canonize the oven were in vain. As with the dinner, I was simply too old. The Ginnies went up on the shelf, along with the useless cardboard appliance.

This is where the McIhenny twins enter the story. The following summer I began baby-sitting for them, my first real job. When my mother and Mrs. McIhenny wanted a chance to talk privately at the McIhennys' house, I was given a dollar to watch the twins at our house. That left only Mrs. McIhenny's three year old and her newborn, and they were too young to understand or repeat what they heard. This was important since, unbeknownst to me at the time, most of the conversations were about Mr. McIhenny, a polar bear of a man with carrot-red hair. The meanest man on our street. None of us ever cut through his yard of weeds and littered appliances because he would yell or chase us out. A mean drunk. Rumor had it among the neighborhood children that he killed off unwanted litters of kittens by cramming stones up their anuses. The parents whispered behind closed doors about stranger, more adult atrocities. While it seemed my mother had little time for me or my brother, she seemed to have endless concern and time for the women in our neighborhood. The neighborhood crusader, the righter of wrongs, my mother was rarely alone. And Mrs. McIhenny seemed to be her most important cause.

The twins, Patsy and Colleen, almost six years old with matching curly red hair (rich and rusty thick then) and freckle-smeared faces, were no problem to watch. Accustomed to the tyranny of their father, they always did exactly what they were told. I liked them. They followed me and seemed to admire everything I did. I particularly enjoyed inventing games for them. The title of baby-sitter allowed me to lose myself in the world of childish invention with complete impunity from the criticism of my peers.

That summer afternoon—the one that just returned to me, so lucid among other faded memories—we were searching for something to do when Colleen pulled Bonita and my oven from my shelf.

"Do these go together?" she asked. "The oven seems kinda big for this doll."

"No," I said. The phone rang. I left the room to answer it—my mother calling to tell me to give the girls plain saltines rather than Oreos with their Kool-Aid, to reseal the waxed-paper mouth of the cracker wrapping. (Where did my brain ever find space to store such a trivial detail, keep safe the very feel of the wax wrapping of the crackers rolling back? As clear as Bonita's ice-blue eyes.) When I returned to my room, I found the girls had placed the oven in the middle of the rug. They had placed Bonita inside so that only her plastic face and upper chest showed through the open oven door. Her eyelids, designed to shut when she reclined, were closed so that the banks of black lashes rested against her cheeks. Like mourners, Colleen and Patsy knelt on either side of the oven.

Gripped by the scene, I paused in the doorway.

"She's dead," I said. As the words came out, they seemed true. Poor Bonita was dead and the oven with the solitary door, drawn back like the top of a Dutch door to reveal only her head and upper torso, was her strange coffin. Even her pealing skin and balding scalp—evidence of long suffering prior to her demise—contributed to the scene's credibility.

"Dead?" asked Patsy, her little-girl eyes wide and bright.

"Yes," I said grimly. "And we must have her funeral."

Thus our game for the afternoon was born. Since funeral was a new game, with no established rules, it had an organic quality that made it more compelling than our regular amusements. The activity was more involved, more real. As I invented each new component, I felt driven, controlled by a greater power. We dressed in my mother's clothing, like true mourners, in a trance. When we twirled around in front of the mirror, we weren't girls playing dress-up, we were preparing for an event, a solemn, serious event. We wore only black. Patsy wore a black slip skirt, pulled up over her flat breasts. Colleen wore a black camisole that reached her knees. And as leader, high priestess, grand inventor, I wore my mother's short black cocktail dress, trimmed in sparkling black sequins, a dress she donned only on special occasions (with matching sequins sprinkled in her hair, a look that nearly rivaled Helena Driscoll). I made shawls for the girls out of large swatches of black fabric found near my mother's sewing machine. We all wore long necklaces, and doilies on our heads.

When we were dressed, I instructed the girls to kneel with me around Bonita's coffin.

"We must mourn," I said in my new grim voice.

"What's that?" asked Patsy.

"Cry, act sad over Bonita's death."

I started and they copied me. At first, our cries were tentative, then artificial—"boo hoos" and "wahhhs"—children's mimics of cartoons. But somewhere among these stages, our cries became real. At what precise point, I can't say. But gradually we were wailing, howling, shaking, screaming, sobbing. I was consumed by a deep and beautiful anguish I had never before experienced. Anguish over Bonita's death, over the sad little oven, over Debbie Driscoll's future, over the twins' mother, the McIhennys' litters of kittens, over the way my mother ignored me, over how very alone I felt I would always be. The twins' tears were far more disturbing than my own. Rather than springing from vague self-pity or sentimentality, their tears seemed to stem from a real terror. Their faces were puffy and pink, slick with tears. Their little shoulders shook.

I knew that as the baby-sitter, the responsible party, I should call an end to the game, comfort the girls, restore the situation to normalcy. Yet I was too in love with my tears, my sadness, the luxury of relinquishing all self-control. I had never felt such complete and utter grief, such total self-indulgence, such knowledge of all my losses, such *ecstasy*. My sobs seized me to the bone, the very marrow; my entire body, my heart, my lungs, every cell, every atom, was crying. I grew scared for myself and for the girls. But the pain was too exhilarating to stop—I loved my agony.

Somehow, between wrenching sobs, I managed to clasp the little coffin between my hands and lift it above my head, as if offering a sacrifice to the gods.

"Agagodoforada," moaned a primitive voice from deep inside me. The rush of sounds emerging from my lips seemed wholly appropriate for the occasion. No real words would have sufficed, could have illustrated my rapture.

Still holding the coffin above my head, I rose. First one foot, then the other. The girls followed my example.

"Agaodohafta, megamontee, agodo," I said as I followed my lifted offering out the door. The three of us formed a wailing procession, down the hallway—I stopped briefly in the bathroom to anoint Bonita's brow (it seemed right)—across the living room, out the front door, down the concrete-slab steps, across the front yard, the sidewalk, across the tree lawn, the curb, right into the middle of the street, where we turned and headed down the block. Where were the neighbors? The mothers? The other children? Did what we were doing really seem to be an innocent game not to be disturbed? Or had we managed to tune everything else out so thoroughly that the world around us ceased to exist? We seemed the only living beings on Barberry, creatures with a mission.

Our thundering grief propelled us, as if prearranged, to the last house on the block. In fact, as we veered up the drive, I realized this was our destination all along: the Trimble house, a prim white saltbox. Until recently, the house had been the smallest on the street, the front almost the same size as the enormous American flag they hung out every Fourth of July and Memorial Day. But a few months ago the Trimbles had started an addition on the rear of their house that was larger than the house itself. The old house looked like a truck cab pulling an enormous load. From all the work, the yard was completely obliterated, flattened by cement trucks and trampled by workmen. But now that the addition was nearing completion, Mr. Trimble had rototilled the backyard in order—according to my father—to put down "sod."

We traipsed up their gravel drive, lifting our legs high so that our black garments didn't trip us, around to the backyard, the freshly rototilled dirt. Still sobbing, we fell to our knees in the fresh Ohio earth. Where was Mrs. Trimble? Her two sons? The youngest, Albert, had spent the entire summer walking up and down the drive with a quarter pressed into his belly button to train it to become an inny rather than an outy. His brother, Herm, was so possessive of their property that he charged us to watch the cement trucks pour their thick and gritty batter into the new room's foundation. How could the neighborhood have been so empty, abandoned? Perhaps the memory has been buried so long that the peripheral images have faded, but that doesn't explain why the other details are so vivid, why no one interrupted our bizarre performance.

The ground was loose and easy to move, moist and malleable clumps that I could easily dig and lift. As we dug, my tears subsided. By the time we had a hole one foot deep and one foot wide, my anguish was replaced with anger. Mounting, inexplicable fury. I placed Bonita's coffin in the grave, closed the oven door, and pushed dirt over the cardboard, refilling the hole. Clenching my teeth, I patted the surface into a neatly pressed mound, and sat back on my haunches. The twins were still sobbing. Seeing them shake and cry annoyed me. I was irritated with myself for not stopping the game when it was obviously provoking inappropriate feelings. And I was pained by the state of my mother's garments. I didn't move, just sat there watching Colleen blubber until Patsy managed to choke out an appeal.

"Please, Alice, dig her up. We've got to dig her up. She can't breathe!"

Her desperation snapped me.

"Shut up!" I yelled, ashamed even as I said it. "She's just a doll, stupid."

The twins immediately quit crying. Colleen gave one final whimper, a little tremor that ran through her body like an aftershock. My tone must have reminded them of their father.

"Come on," I said. "We've got to get out of here before the Trimbles get home."

We walked back to my house on the sidewalk. Neighbors roamed the street now. Mothers. Dogs. Cats. Children. The world had returned. I rinsed off my mother's slip and camisole and stuffed them in the washing machine. I scrubbed the damp knee marks I'd made on her dress and hung it back up in the closet, hoping the stains vanished by the next time she needed it. In the bathroom, we scrubbed dirt from our hands, watching the muddy water swirl down the drain, and cleaned beneath our nails with toothpicks. Presentable again, we sat in the kitchen drinking Kool-Aid and munching saltines. We were still sitting there when my mother returned with Mrs. McIhenny, one child clinging to her shirttail, the other riding a hip.

"What did you do?" my mother asked in the perfunctory remote voice she always used with me. I wasn't a woman with problems.

"Nothing," I said.

"You mean Alice didn't think up any of her clever games for you girls?" Mrs. McIhenny asked, a smile plastered on her blotchy face. She had been crying.

Colleen shrugged and took another saltine. Patsy licked salt off the surface of her cracker.

"Okay, well, just play deaf and dumb if it makes you happy. But we'd better get a move on if I'm going to have dinner on the table before your father gets home."

At the mention of their father, both girls popped off their chairs. Before Mrs. McIhenny led her brood out the door, my mother touched her arm—such a loving gesture!—and said, "Call if you need me. Neil can watch the kids."

Mrs. McIhenny smiled wanly and nodded, but didn't look back once she was out the door.

My mother went about her business as if she was alone which, for her, I'm sure was the case. I was left haunted by memories of the twins' startled faces when I snapped. Already, I was ashamed of the way I'd treated them, ashamed of what I'd done to Bonita.

I must have planned to go dig her up. I'm sure I did. I could have given her to the twins. They had so few toys. But once the spell dissolved, it was not so easy to think of marching into the Trimbles' yard, dealing with Herm Trimble. So as it often is with summers, one day turned into the next and then the next, without any clear demarcation. Yet I'm sure I would have found the right time if it weren't for the sod.

Walking home from swimming lessons one hazy afternoon I spotted the long flatbed truck in front of the Trimble house. Despite instructions, I had worn my wet bathing suit under my clothes. I was damp and uncomfortable. The crotch was riding up my rear end. I wanted to change. Yet I stopped to join the circle of children watching the action in the Trimbles' backyard. I even paid an extra nickel to shoulder my way to the front. Sod was not what I thought—seeds from pods sprinkled on the ground—rather, it was a thick carpet of grass. The yard had been leveled to receive the lush rug. Men rolled it out in strips. My throat tightened.

Bonita gone, buried forever in an unmarked grave.

My brother, Tim, appears at my car window.

"Is that you, Alice?" he asks. His voice is gentle, grown, not the voice of the teasing boy I remember. "There are so many cars here that I didn't notice you in this rented one until just now. You shouldn't be outside by yourself. Come on inside."

Streetlights glow in the dusk. How long have I been here?

Tim opens the door. Stiffly, I stretch my legs and follow him into the house. Both the living-room coffee table and the dining-room table are covered with dishes: casseroles, salads, breads, pies. The room is so packed with bodies, mostly women, that it's hard to breathe. A broad woman with a head of Brillo Pad–gray hair hugs me; I feel the wrench of her shoulders. The silent crying. "You poor thing," she says. I want to tell her that she probably knew my mother better than I, but I don't. Yes, we chatted on the phone: my mother sharing news of her friends' troubles, their illnesses, their husbands' deaths, the plights of their grown children. Every few years she flew out to visit me and her grandchildren for a week. But we seldom really talked, and she *never* listened. That doesn't mean I'm bitter. Now that I am a mother myself I know that a person can be good, warm and kind even, without necessarily being a wonderful mother. Look at all these people she helped.

I watch the women in the room comforting one another, and I think of the mothers I knew—Mrs. Driscoll, Mrs. McIhenny, Mrs. Trimble—all buried inside grandmothers. Across the room, I see the McIhenny twins, their freckles faded so that their little-girl faces live only in cracking old photographs now. I think of my mother. Then I think of Bonita. I see the ground cut away, the earth's layers revealed like a side of sliced cake. I see a strip of green-green grass, a layer of thick brown dirt, the wall of the oven, and then Bonita inside the oven—the sway of her plastic belly, her blue glass eyes, her tiny fingernails—and find relief that she, at least, is forever preserved.

A Position of Trying

My brother Murph says his house is full of rats. He jokes about it. When he first moved in, Murph said he knew there were rodents only because of the droppings. But later, he claimed, the rats got bolder. Murph would walk in a room and see the flicker of a tail as one disappeared beneath a piece of furniture. And now, *he says*, the rats hardly notice him at all. They'll saunter in a room, select their meal right off his plate, then sashay right back out.

That's why I'm sitting out here on the porch. And why my boys, Brian Jr. and Francis, are playing in the patch of earth between here and the toolshed. I won't let them near the woodpile for fear of rats. Oh sure, I know my brother exaggerates. His "rats" may very well be field mice. Murph probably just likes to tell the story, imitating the rats, sashaying limp-wristed out of the room. But still, I feel better waiting for Murph out here on his porch.

All my brothers exaggerate. They love to tell stories, to joke and act wild. Being the youngest and the only girl, I was teased a lot. They're that way because of our father. He was the biggest prankster of them all. I cringe when I think of his humor, always finding amusement in his own misfortunes. The worst time, the time that actually makes me sick when I think about it, was Christmas morning the year I was sixteen. After we opened our presents, Daddy read us a copy of Great Aunt Mary Patricia's Last Will and Testament. She was our rich aunt who'd died Christmas Eve morning. Daddy was sitting on the ottoman under the Christmas tree, laughing his head off while he read it. I can still see his face, red and contorted, the vein on his forehead bulging, forking out over his eyes like those rivers on the U.S. relief map that hung over my brother Kevin's bed. Daddy went through what seemed like a hundred one-thousand-dollar endowments. Then he came to Uncle Brad:

> And to my dear nephew, Bradford Thomas Murphy, who self-lessly cared for me during the years of my illness, I give, devise and bequeath ten thousand dollars and any and all property that is not now or subsequently allocated.

Then, laughing so hard he could barely read, he came to himself:

> And to my nephew, Francis Sean Murphy, I give, devise and bequeath one hundred dollars and the GE clock radio he gave me for my seventieth birthday.

I was very quiet. Even my brothers, who'd been laughing all along, became quiet.

"Don't you get it?" asked my father, leaning forward, waving his copy of the will. "Don't you see? Mary Patricia was senile. She got us confused. *I* was the one who took care of her while she was sick. Brad gave her the clock radio."

Then my brothers began to howl, rolling forward, beating the floor with their fists.

I fingered the cuff on one of my new boots. I'd just opened them. They were still resting on a bed of tissue in the box: leather and fitted. I'd wanted them all year. They cost over forty dollars. I couldn't forget that since mother had been saying it all month; *Now remember, Jane, if you get those boots that'll be it, nothing else.* Next to Uncle Brad's ten thousand dollars, the boots seemed like nothing.

"Daddy," I said, "couldn't you try to—what do they call it—contest the will?"

He wiped the tears of laughter from his eyes and looked at me. "I could *try.*" But his emphasis on the word stressed its uselessness. He and Uncle Brad had had an argument and hadn't spoken in years. Uncle Brad would rather burn the money than share it with Daddy.

The will: that was only the beginning of the joke. Brad, as executor, was supposed to arrange the funeral, but he was vacationing in

Florida and no one knew where. So Daddy had to do everything. Only the new director at the funeral home wouldn't embalm the body without a telegram with Brad's signature on it. So what did Daddy do? He sent a singing telegram and signed Brad's name:

Mary P is dead
   dead dead dead
Bury her deep
   deep deep deep

It cost him almost his entire inheritance, but to him and my brothers, it was worth it. Even now, Murph, the brother I'm waiting for, loves to tell the story. My husband, Brian, says he's heard it at least fifty times down at the bar.

That's where Murph probably is now, the bar. He stops there every day after work, but usually only for a beer or two unless it's payday which today isn't. I hope he gets here soon. Brian Jr. and Francis are getting messy. There isn't any grass in this yard, only hard ground covered with a fine layer of dirt. Brian Jr. and Francis are racing little metal cars, Hot Wheels, that plow through the dirt, leaving trails. They sit on one foot and twirl around, so that the cars make big circles around them. Brian Jr.—he's five, the oldest—sometimes leans forward and makes a road by sweeping his hand through the dirt. I can see the dust rise and fall, settling on his arms and hair. He has a crew cut. We had to get him one; he had so many cowlicks that there was no combing it. But now, to my surprise, I actually like it. His hair is so thick that it makes me think of red velvet. I love to run my open palm over it. My husband's friends don't like it: *Hey man*, they say to Brian, *why'd you wanna go and make your kid look like a redneck?* The funny thing is (funny meaning weird) that even with their long hair, they're all rednecks and don't even know it.

I wish Murph would hurry up. If he doesn't, there'll be no stopping the boys from climbing in the woodpile.

I can imagine Murph's face when I tell him I'm leaving Brian. He won't believe me at first. He'll think it's a joke. Then he'll get mad, demand to hear my reasons, threaten to call Brian. It's not that he and Brian are even friends. But they've known each other a long time and both work at the tool-and-die where Daddy used to be head foreman, so they've developed a mutual respect. But in the end that won't matter much. Murph will give in. Blood is thicker than water. He'll lend me some money and call our oldest brother, Russ, and convince him to let me come and stay with him for a while. I know how it all will happen, but it tires me to think of actually going through the motions. The air is so fresh tonight, springlike, that I just want to start driving to Russ's right away. Maybe, even though I probably could make it in one night, we'll stop at a motel. If there are lawn chairs at the motel's pool, maybe, after the boys go to sleep, I'll drag one up by our room and sit outside by myself. I could have a Coke and listen to the crickets. That's one of the things about living in a second-floor apartment with babies—you don't get to hear night noises much. But it's not easy for young people to buy a house.

If only I didn't have to go through the motions. Even when Murph calls Russ there'll be jokes. Maybe he'll disguise his voice, pretend like he's a disc jockey or some big-time lawyer calling to tell Russ he's won a million bucks, before he gets down to the real business.

It's those jokes, those awful jokes, that made me like Brian in the first place. I even met Brian during one of my brothers' jokes. It was after Russ had lost four of his fingers at the cannery, but before he'd moved out of Middleview. He and Murph and some of their friends were going to the Moonlite Drive-in. Mother made them take me along. She thought it would keep them out of trouble (ha-ha). Russ made me pretend I was his date in the front while Murph and the others (Brian among them) hid under the tarp in the back. We got in okay and parked up near the front (Russ said that would be less suspicious than if we hid out in the back row) and all the guys came out from beneath the tarp. I can still remember how everything looked. We were up so close that the pores on Gregory Peck's nose looked as big as plums. There weren't many cars there that night so the unattached speaker poles spread out behind us like the crosses in that photo of Arlington Cemetery that the *Middleview Eagle* prints every Memorial Day. We hadn't been sitting there ten minutes before the Moonlite parking lot superintendent approached us and asked to see our ticket stubs. Well Russ, he just sat there, next to me, and stared back at the superintendent. We were all getting real tense in that silence until finally Russ said, *So you wanna see my stubs, eh buddy,* then he thrust out the hand that had been eaten up in his press at the cannery, sticking his mangled finger stubs right in the superintendent's face. Shit. That man's face turned so pale that it looked like he was going to be sick. Murph, leaning over the seat, was trying so hard not to laugh, his cheeks bloated and his whiskers standing straight out, that he looked like one of those puffer fish we saw on the sixth grade field trip to the natural history museum. I really felt for that superintendent. I mean, what could he do? He just kind of slunk away, backwards, and never bothered us again. It was funny to everyone else. But to me it was sad. When I glanced in the backseat, I saw that Brian wasn't laughing either—he and I were the only ones not laughing. It was some time after that—I'm not sure exactly when—that we began seeing each other.

Next to my family, Brian seemed very serious. He'd had the most miserable, serious childhood I'd ever heard of. His house had burned down and both his little brother and daddy had died in the flames. Brian drove me by the house once. All the windows and doors were boarded over. The wood above them was charred black, thick streaks created by escaping flames tapered up and outward from each of the corners—like shadowy arms of screaming spirit women. Brian told me what the house was like when he lived in it. But still, as I sat there looking at it from his car, I pictured Brian living in that house the way it was as I looked at it—the long grass and weeds flattened to a tangled mat by years of wind and rain and neglect. I didn't see the homemade patio where Brian said he took his father bottles of beer and can openers before there were flip tops. Instead I saw his father sitting in an aluminum-and-mesh lawn chair, crooked on top of the uneven weeds. I imagined the little brother running, trying to hide, but the matted grass was too firmly pressed to the ground to crawl behind. I envisioned the father's wooden leg, the one that replaced the real one he had lost after jumping from a train as a boy, propped up. I envisioned the silver coins Brian said were pounded into the leg. Sometimes, Brian said, his father let him and his brother take turns—pounding so many coins that in my mind, I saw the leg glimmer in the sunlight. Thinking of all this gave me a chill, but it made me like Brian all the more.

Not that I ever would have married someone just because he was serious—had I known what I was doing. But I didn't figure it out until the very moment the priest, Father Ted, was reading our vows. My hair was almost to my waist then. It was pulled back with the band of little satin roses that held my veil in place. My gown had a lace-and-satin bodice with off-the-shoulder sleeves. We had a big wedding. I had six bridesmaids all in powder blue and all the ushers wore powder blue velveteen tuxedos. I was surveying how pretty everything looked out of the corner of my eye when I noticed Murph snickering at Kevin and Russ. Then I saw Brian staring at Father Ted in such a serious way that the spattering of freckles around his eyes stood out. And in a flash, I knew all my motives. Just like that, I knew I was marrying him to get away from my family and enter the serious world of other people.

And in that same flashy sort of way, it came to me a year later, when Brian Jr. was born, that Brian wasn't serious. He was just sad, sad, sad. Ever so sad. But I in my childlike ways had mistaken sadness for seriousness. I just figured it out while he was sitting next to me on my bed. He was the only one in his family to come visit me and our new baby in the hospital. Both his father and his brother were dead. And his mother had remarried and gone off to live in Wisconsin. My relatives had been coming in and out all day. It was so sad. How could I have been so naive!

I can't share that sadness with him anymore.

Brian Jr. is pouring dirt in Francis's hair. I hope it doesn't get in his eyes. He'll cry. I would say something, but shit, it's washable. Besides, I think they've forgotten about me. I don't want to remind them or they'll start nagging me about when Murph is going to get here.

I couldn't even stand the sadness of telling Brian I was leaving him. I'd planned to, but fifteen minutes before he came home, I pulled all our things out of the suitcases and stuffed them in Pick-N-Pay bags. I told him I had to go to the grocery store to pick up something for dinner. The shopping bags? I said they were filled with old baby clothes that I was going to stuff in the Salvation Army bin behind the Pick-N-Pay. Right now he is probably thinking, *I thought she was going to pick up something for dinner, not do the whole damn week's grocery shopping.* He's probably rehearsing the way he'll say it to me when I return. It will be a while yet before he gets worried. And later, when Murph calls, he'll be mad. He's not the violent type, but when he realizes I've taken our only car, he'll probably punch a wall. I can imagine the dent. Unless it's the kitchen wall, which is drywall. His fist will go clean through that. I can see the hole, puckering like a big kiss, when he pulls his hand back out.

It's funny (funny meaning weird again) how all my realizations come to me at monumental moments like weddings and births. It was at my father's funeral that I figured out I'd be leaving Brian. It was nothing he did. It was my brothers. Except for my wedding, I'd never seen them all dressed up like that in one place. At the service it was okay; their eyes watered like everyone else's. But afterwards at the wake, they were as wild as ever. It didn't even seem believable that they'd managed to get there on their own. I imagined a cowboy riding through Middleview, swinging his lasso, roping them all and stuffing them in their suits and ties. And it was at that moment— when I saw that picture in my head—that I figured it all out. Their wildness, funniness, was just like Brian's seriousness—nothing but a cover for sadness. The moment I knew that, I knew I'd be leaving. I knew I'd take the boys and go to Russ's. But I won't be there for long; we'll be out on our own soon.

Even with the rats, Murph is lucky to have this house. He gets to stay here for free. It belongs to Red Williams, the plant manager down at the tool-and-die. The state is going to rip it down soon to build a highway and Red will get more money if he can prove he's been using the house. They're going to pretend Murph has been paying him two hundred dollars a month for rent. I can see it all now. An enormous truck with a ball and chain will come. The ball will crash into the house, making it slant in one direction while the rats, like a rodent army from the Saturday morning cartoons, will march away in the other direction.

But I don't like sitting here, thinking about the house. Every time I think about a house it reminds me of Brian's burning house, his father's wooden leg. All through our marriage that leg has haunted me. The heaviness of that leg is why, the firemen said, Brian's father couldn't get out in time. They said he was found in a position of trying. The little brother was hiding under a bed. I don't want to be found in any position; I want to be gone.

It'll be a relief to see Murph's red truck flying through the trees, up the dirt road, past the 7-Eleven; Brian Jr. and Francis are getting too bored to wait much longer. Francis just threw one of his Hot Wheels. They'll be fighting soon. But even though they bicker, I'm glad I had two boys before I realized I'd be leaving Brian. That way they'll have each other—because they'll never *really* have me.

The Call of Private Ghosts

"**I** don't know, Ma," said Will with a sigh. "I don't think she's the one for me, you know? She overreacts."

"Like how?" asked Mary, the portable phone tucked under her chin as she lifted the colander from the sink. She shook the metal container back and forth, jarring loose excess water, like sifting for gold.

"She imagines things," said Will.

"Ohhh?" moaned Mary, fitting the colander back in the sink.

"No, not like that," he snorted, evincing mild disgust. He was serious. He didn't want teasing or banter.

"Okay then be specific, give me an example." Her words were familiar, the same prompts she had used to illicit symptoms when he was an ill toddler, to generate sentences when he wrote his first junior high essays, to help him through his troubled teens, and, now, in their cross-country conversations.

"Well, at this party, she thought this guy was eyeing her. She got real, you know, paranoid. It embarrassed me. I mean she had to tell everyone she saw that he was after her or something."

"Well, maybe he was." Still cradling the phone, Mary poured herself another quarter-glass of wine.

"No, it was just 'cause the guy was naked and she . . ."

"Naked?"

"It's not like that, no big deal, it was a hot night. The party was along a river. Probably some people were skinny-dipping . . ."

"Was everyone naked?"

"No, just this guy, you're not listening. Maybe they were in the river, but he was the only one trotting around naked," said Will. "So Penny got it in her head he was after her."

Many years had passed since Mary attended a party where nudity was considered normal. She remembered one, when Will was about four, and two college girls were cooking in the kitchen, stripped from the waist up. No big deal. A perfectly hip thing to do on a hot night. But it had bothered Mary to see them acting so normal, their bare breasts bobbing as they shifted sizzling frying pans and lugged big vats of vegetarian chili to the table. She remembered one girl had knotted little pink nipples while the other's sepia-colored aureoles were as soft and spread as poached eggs. She recalled little else about the party except that Will had slept upstairs on someone's waterbed. She remembered sitting down next to him when it was time to leave, the way the partially filled mattress sent a slow wave across the surface, moving Will out of her reach. The rise and fall of his small body as the ripple carried him away.

"*Ma*, you're not listening."

"Yes, I am. I was thinking that it isn't so strange to be uncomfortable with a naked man you don't know."

"At a huge party?"

Mary felt the rush of warmth she always experienced when Will sought her motherly opinion. Too many of their years had been spent like siblings. Playing together, but bickering as well. She always felt an undercurrent, that if she said the wrong thing, he could be swept away forever. After all, they only had each other holding them together, no other links. But when he wanted her advice, she felt like a regular television mother, a Brady mom, albeit one who gave advice about a naked man at a party. Still, it was something.

She took a sip of wine.

"Sure, besides, Penny is from a small town in Iowa. Her first time away from home, right?"

"That's another thing. Penny," he spit the word out. "That name."

Mary laughed. For as long as she could remember Will had a sensitivity to language, with a particular aversion to words that started with *P*. Petunia. Potato. He seemed to resent the effort he had to put into each word, as if language should be at his command, not the other way around. Mary heard the jangle of keys in the front door of the house.

"I think Sam's here," she said.

"At least he has a decent name," said Will. Will liked Sam, a rare occurrence in Mary's series of men since Will's father had taken off. "How is he doing?"

"Good; tired like all of us."

"All you old fogies, that is," said Will, teasing in that television-child way that Mary loved. As if they were a real family, with problems no more serious than generation gaps.

"Remember, I'm only eighteen years ahead of you."

"I'll age better; I won't have a kid to stress me out."

Sam entered the kitchen. A big man with broad shoulders and a lush beard as thick as pile carpeting, he filled the doorway. His eyebrows, as full and dark as his beard, peaked over his intense eyes like little thatched roofs. When Will first met him, he had whispered to Mary, "Looks like Satan to me." But no one was gentler than Sam.

Sam kissed Mary on top of her head and plucked a carrot slice from the salad.

"Look, Will, I've got to go finish making dinner. We need to make plans for spring break, your reservations and all."

"Yeah, Easter or Passover? You gonna make me a basket?"

"We'll see. I'll talk to you later. I love you."

Mary's father had been Jewish, her mother Catholic. Will's father, Billy, had been Catholic, now Sam was Jewish. Mary had lived a secular Christian life until Will was twelve. Christmas trees and Easter baskets. Then, exactly ten years ago, Mary began practicing a sort of secular Judaism. She saw this as part of the process of assimilating herself with her past, bringing together all the scattered segments of her life, of being more honest about her real self.

"Will?" asked Sam as he pulled a stool up to the tiny cutting-board island and Mary hung up the phone. His intense eyes bore into her. "Did you tell him?"

The words struck her. She had forgotten there was anything to tell until just now.

"No. He had stuff he needed to talk about."

"Are you going to tell him?"

She shrugged. "I don't want to talk about it now."

For as long as Mary could remember, she had lived two lives simultaneously: a real life and an imagined life, running along side

THE CALL OF PRIVATE GHOSTS 73

by side, the authentic life having no more weight than the other. In fact, in ways, the private life, the imagined life, was more powerful— the same way her father's Judaism, acknowledged by little more than a tiny mezuzah hung by the front door and an affirmative nod if asked, had more of a draw than the Catholicism which surrounded her both in practice and by icons (along with crosses hung everywhere, her mother kept a three-foot-high Madonna atop her bedroom dresser, votive candles on the sideboard in the dining room, and a whimsically soft and Aryan-looking painting of Jesus over the kitchen table).

Mary's imagined life always seemed to emerge in direct contrast to her real life. When her mother took her to church, she never saw herself as a Catholic, rather as a Jew in disguise. When she was a girl, she always lived in her head as if she were a woman, blocking out the tedium of childhood with visions of herself as a sophisticated grown-up. She sat aside at many a birthday party imagining the cosmopolitan entertaining she would do as an adult, well-deserved respites from all her good works in the jungles of South America. Visions of her adult life were as tangible as the scratches on her sixth-grade desk. When Will's birth (Willy as she called him until he was fifteen) made the adult life she had expected impossible, Mary hardly noticed. Instead she switched course, constructing a pretend life with Will that she imagined would be true when her ship came in. Even as they sat in their tiny apartment over the dry cleaners, the steam rising from the pants press keeping them warm since they couldn't afford heating the apartment above sixty degrees, Mary saw Willy in wool shorts and kneesocks, à la John-John Kennedy, waving as he boarded a plane for Eaton. Later when she first received her LPN license, she was surprised when people at the hospital called her "nurse," as she was so actively a physician in her head. But now that passing out meds and changing cath bags had become such undeniable reality, the life that ran next to her actual one was her past, the life she had already lived but paid so little attention to because her imagined future consumed all her time.

This new imagined world was peopled with ghosts from the past, the residue of people as they had once existed. Mary had a chance to have what she missed, correct old wrongs. She had conversations with old high school friends standing beside their lockers, the rows of dented gray doors as lucid and familiar as the intensity in Sam's eyes. But most important, she gave Willy all the time and attention he needed. She had been so misguided when he was young. Now, in her imagined world, instead of including a first-grade Willy—long after night had descended—in deciding dinner plans as if he were an equal, she would shop early in the day. Cook healthy meals. In her mind's eye, she cleaned and chopped vegetables daily, made soups that simmered for hours. And Billy, Willy's father, was there, traveling life with her, offering support, helping her with decisions, being the father Willy hadn't seen since he was two. The genuine quality of this imagined life was what enabled her to remain unsurprised when, after nearly twenty years of silence, she heard his voice on the other end of the phone line.

"I'm looking for my son."

Sam rolled from his back to his side and Mary followed suit. From above, she imagined they looked like two people standing in line, perhaps a conga dance line, Sam's large hand draped loosely across the notch of her waist. Soon, he gently snored, the sound of sleep, and Mary was alone, the room drenched in a murky darkness. The furniture outlines were still visible, but only through a veil of gray pointillism. The tall dresser, across from the bed, was the same one she had shared with Billy, the same one her mother had owned when she was alive. Mary stared at it, trying to summon the details from the monochromatic gray bulk—the sharp edges, the chipped drawers, the brass knobs gummy with ancient dirt. If she tried hard enough, she might be able to discern the features of the tall Madonna—her outspread arms, her parted lips, her sad eyes, her long, ghostly white robe—even though she hadn't graced the dresser in many, many years. As a girl, Mary had viewed the Madonna as an older woman, one who dutifully gave up her grown son with little emotion. Now Mary saw her as another mother, one stricken by the loss of her son, his age of no consequence.

When Mary was seventeen and Billy was twenty, they ran away together in his souped-up Chevy. They traveled as far as they could from southern Illinois—tires spinning, hot tar bubbles popping, spraying gravel on dusty back roads—to California where they spent what seemed, in retrospect, like fifteen minutes in the tumultuous California scene before Mary found herself pregnant and they headed back to southern Illinois. In their hometown of East Well, near

Carbondale, they were famous for another fifteen minutes before most of Mary's friends went off to college and Billy got a job, with his best friend, at a muffler shop.

"Billy?"

"Bill, now. I want my son, Bill Jr."

"Willy."

"You still call him *that*?" Disgust was evident in his tone. Mary was surprised. Hadn't he always been warm in her imagined conversations? And why would *he* be angry? Wasn't he the one who had skipped out on child support?

"Well, yes, though we dropped the *y*; it's just Will now," she admitted grudgingly, not liking the fact that both Will and Bill had dropped the *y*, an implied bond that excluded her. She considered telling Bill her name was Mar now, but quickly dismissed the idea.

"He's not here. He grew up. Did you think he would still be here, waiting in his playpen?" Her voice assumed a tone she hadn't used in years. Sarcasm. The same voice she had used in arguments with him when he arrived home hours after the muffler shop had closed. Where had that voice been hiding all those years? How had it come forth so readily, so easily?

"I know how old he is. I need to see him, talk to him." He paused. "I'm sick. I need to see him now."

Mary wondered if the last part was a lie. Billy was such a liar. She had forgotten that part of him: the stories he made up when he came home from the muffler shop so late. The old woman he said he helped on the road. The runaway teenager he volunteered to drive all the way back home to Chicago.

"I can't just give you his number without asking him first. He may not be interested after all these years." She suddenly wanted Billy to think Will was still nearby, not reveal any clues that he was far away in college in Arizona. She added casually, "What's your number? I'll give it when I see him."

"See him soon," Billy said. When Mary had the number, seven actual digits with an unfamiliar area code, she thought maybe Billy was telling her the truth.

After Billy deserted her and Willy, Mary's life had splintered even more. She could barely keep track of all her lives, who she was at any given time. In addition to her imagined existences, she lived two external lives. She fell in with a crowd at Southern Illinois University in Carbondale. Though she didn't take any classes at the university, she attended their parties, hung out at the houses they shared, like the one where the topless girls served chili. She played the part of a free spirit with a love child, alluded to her days in California in a way that made it sound more like years than weeks. She resembled the students in her gauzy Indian tops, her hair roping past her shoulders, Willy riding her hip dressed in bib overalls. But while her imagined lives always seemed real, this life felt fraudulent. They were college kids. She was the ex-wife of an auto mechanic. With them she ate vegetarian and drank watery teas, but at home, eleven miles away in East Well, she scarfed down juicy cheeseburgers, guzzled Cokes, rewarded Will for his potty training efforts with M&Ms, while dreaming of the perfect house, Willy frolicking in the halls in his wool shorts and kneesocks.

Mary can't remember what prompted her to take her first course—Human Spirituality—or when she sent away for grant applications. Her dad helped some, but Mary's mother's lingering death had left him with enormous bills. The stuffing had been let out of him, like a sack with a slow leak. He was the same man, only three sizes smaller, cheeks that used to be puffy collapsed against hollow cheekbones. Mary didn't like burdening him with her needs.

She spent three years at Southern Illinois University before moving up to Chicago to get her LPN, a practical means for supporting Willy. There, in the tiny apartment over the dry cleaners, she practiced giving injections to pieces of fruit. Late at night, the apartment was dark except for the glow of her gooseneck lamp, as she memorized the parts of the body. Then, once she had her LPN, she studied Judaism by the same lamp. Through it all, Willy, in her mind's eye, outgrew his wool shorts and kneesocks, and became a preppie dressed in Levi's and crew-neck sweaters; no matter that he only donned this attire when her father came up to visit for a weekend. That's how *she* saw him, not how he dressed the rest of the time, like a punk, all black, coming home hours after school had dismissed, his arrival announced by the caustic sound of his skateboard wheels whirling to a stop on the sidewalk in front of the dry cleaners.

Mary had been reading about Sukkoth, the Jewish festival of booths, one late afternoon when the buzzer rang. It was already dark outside, but Mary hadn't bothered to flip on the light because she had read only a few pages before slipping into an imagined life, one where she and Willy built a Sukkoth on the back porch overlooking the dry cleaners' parking lot. She imagined them working together, pounding boards into place, three nail heads protruding from her pursed lips like a cartoon carpenter. The buzzer shook her free of her reverie. No one ever rang in the afternoon if she wasn't expecting company. Could Willy have forgotten his keys? Mary raced down the narrow stairway to the door. If not for the ugly brown-rubber runner, she would have tripped. When she opened the door, Mary needed a moment to assimilate the situation. Standing outside was a Chicago cop, with a mean face as pasty as a bundt cake. Mary's heart fluttered. What could this mean? Was Willy hurt? But, no he couldn't be; for wasn't that Willy—looking perfectly healthy—whom the cop gripped by his upper left arm, throwing his bony shoulders into a slant, as if he balanced a pole with water buckets?

Mary had stared into Willy's face, and was surprised by who glared back—a pale adolescent, his soaked black clothes clinging to his body, his wet hair slicked back, his slit of a mouth set in a sneer—a person who had both her face *and* Billy's. It was not the way people said. "Oh, you have your mother's eyes and your father's nose."

Willy was not simply a Mr. Potato Head stuck with random features. He had *both* their features, *simultaneously.* As if a transparency of Mary's face had been laid over a photo of Billy's, so that both mouths coexisted, both pairs of eyes. Mary's sharp cheekbones and widow's peak over Billy's square face and distrustful eyes. One face on top of the other.

It turned out that he had cut school; had, in fact, cut school many times. But that day, he and two friends (hoodlums, the cop called them) were caught swimming beneath the secured tarp of a motel swimming pool. It was a miracle no one drowned.

The next day, Mary called her father. He found them a little house on a street that ran parallel to his for less rent than they paid over the dry cleaners. That weekend, they moved back down to East Well. Willy sat scrunched by the car door, snarling that he'd run away forever if she forced him to stay in that hick town. Even though Mary knew all children said such things, the words dug at her core the whole time she drove the perfectly straight and flat road to southern Illinois. She could not imagine anything worse than Willy leaving her.

• • •

Mary liked the night shift best. So few emergencies occurred in East Well that after midnight, while the patients slept, she was pretty much free to do what she wanted. Tonight, she sat at the nurse's station, imagining Laura Williams, her best friend in high school when she started dating Billy. Mary could see Laura as she was then, leaning against the wall by the stainless-steel drinking fountain. A tall girl, with short legs, Laura had a look that made Mary envision a giraffe, particularly when she traipsed down the hallway in her slow, languid way, clutching the books to her chest as if holding herself together. In her mind, when Mary told Laura that Billy had returned, Laura gasped, a sharp intake of breath, the way she always indicated surprise.

"After twenty years? Where does he live?"

"I don't know. All I have is his phone number."

As Mary thought these words to Laura, a light went off in her head. Of course! She could locate Billy's state from the area code listings in the front of the phone book. She reached under the counter of the nurse station for the thin East Well phone book, but couldn't locate it among all the debris—despite all the clean surfaces, no place is messier than a hospital—so she grabbed the big Chicago book and flopped it on the counter. She turned the first tissuelike page. A map of U.S. area codes spread before her. 702. Nevada. Right next to Arizona. She could see Will and Bill, so close on the map, crossing the thick black line that separated the states, visiting frequently, establishing a relationship that excluded Mary, separated by so many black lines, so many borders.

Mary's heart stopped. Her hand cupped the phone to call Laura, then slackened. The Laura she wanted to speak with didn't exist anymore. The grown-up Laura only liked to discuss software, megabytes, and computer hardware. She still gasped when someone conveyed startling news; but the gasp was only a ghostly imitation of her girlish gasp, not evidence of genuine surprise.

Mary stared at the squiggles in the gleaming linoleum floor until one moved, separated from itself, like a shadow deserting its body, a cockroach scurrying across the recently waxed surface to disappear under the dark crack of a patient's door.

Mary met Sam a few years after she moved back to East Well. In Chicago for a visit, he introduced himself at a party, "By the way, my name is Sam." Educated as a mathematician at MIT, Sam worked for a game company. Their resident genius. He developed math games, and figured out point systems for complicated board, card, and computer games. "By the way," Mary came to learn, was his means of approaching any awkward topic. It was as if he could throw off his audience by prefacing questions or comments with a phrase generally reserved for casual utterances. When Mary was leaving the party, he said, "By the way, I was wondering if we could get together sometime."

This one small deception was Sam's only foray into dishonesty. In fact, Mary was struck by the depths of his honesty. She wondered if it was connected to his profession, if a mathematician who dealt continually with the certainty of numbers was given to a purer understanding of honesty. She knew he detested dishonesty in others. His presence prompted Mary to work harder to rid herself of her imagined lives, merge and reconcile her real one. And being with such a honest man helped to eclipse all the dishonest years she spent because of Billy.

The first night they slept together, Sam had nudged her toward the bedroom. She stopped him, saying that she needed to wash the makeup from her face. When she and Laura were in high school, they had read in a women's magazine that for every night a woman didn't cleanse her face, her skin aged two weeks.

When Mary told Sam this, he blinked twice, his huge lids sweeping his intense eyes, a mathematician at work making a swift calculation, and said, "That means a fifteen year old who didn't wash her face at night until she was twenty would age seventy-five years in those five years." Holding each other, they had silently laughed for minutes, Sam's solid belly jiggling comfortingly against hers.

They saw each other every day for the rest of her visit. Afterwards, Sam traveled back and forth between East Well and Chicago. Because he did much of his work at home, it was easy to take long weekends. Now that Will was gone, they were talking about living together. Mary didn't want to leave her father. But neither of them wanted to reside permanently in East Well, so the decision kept getting postponed.

The next time Billy phoned, his call was completely unexpected so Mary's unrehearsed response seemed natural. No. Will did not wish to see him. He had survived all this time without so much as a postcard. No. He didn't care if Bill was sick; who had time for a sick stranger? No. Plain and simple. He didn't want to see Bill. No. And don't try to contact him again.

Mary felt strong when she hung up. Confident. Billy, she realized— at least his specter—was the fear she had been carrying for years, the entity that could come between her and Will, sweep him away. He had been there all those years, just beyond words, right outside their sphere of vision. A ghost haunting their relationship. Even though he had been dead to them for years, as dead as Mary's mother, his draw had been powerful.

Still charged with confidence, Mary lifted the receiver and called Will. The lies flowed effortlessly. "Dead. Your father's dead. I just heard from his new wife." Mary wasn't sure where the wife had come from, but she liked her; the idea of a new family pushed Billy even farther from them.

Will was silent for nearly a full minute before he spoke, "I really believed . . . I always believed I'd have a chance to see him again. To speak to him."

"Oh, honey . . ." said Mary.

"No, it's okay," said Will. "Probably better this way."

Yes, thought Mary, buoyed by his response, it's better. She listened for thirty minutes to Will's memories of his father, a memorial composed of fragmented images—a few words in the bed of a pickup truck, the rusted ridges on the floor of the pickup, the way the hair on the back of Billy's hand was thicker on his knuckles than elsewhere, the way he laughed at Maxwell Smart on television, in a boat somewhere helping Willy steady a homemade fishing pole—so that by the time Mary hung up she was truly sad, in mourning.

When Sam arrived at dusk, she fell into his arms sobbing. He had to prod her for the words, the story of Billy's wife contacting her about his death. Sam called the hospital to say Mary would miss a few days. A death in the family.

That night, Mary covered all the mirrors with her best linen napkins. She remembered the rabbi in Chicago telling her that Jews covered mirrors because vanity wasn't permitted in a time of mourning. But Mary did it simply because she didn't want to see her eyes for a while. Near midnight, she found one of her mother's old candles on the top shelf of a closet, lit it, and put it on her dining room table as her mother would have done. Before she climbed into bed, she poured a little stream of water around the bed. She couldn't remember if the custom was Christian or Jewish or far more primitive, but she knew she had read, somewhere, that ghosts could not cross water without falling in.

Many times in Mary's life, she regretted her words after she spoke, sometimes just seconds later. She wished she could grab them from the air and cram them back down her throat. Other times, she wished she had spent more time planning her remarks. She replayed numerous conversations in her head, deleting, editing, adding, rephrasing. Often for days.

But this time, she had no regrets.

As a result of her actions, Mary felt everything fall into place. She had taken control of both her future and her past. Will called her more frequently. Sam, always gentle, treated her with a new tenderness. All her actions acquired a fresh purpose, became preparations for a real future, not an imagined one or a reinvented past. Her life became one steady line forward. She decided to move to Chicago, to live with Sam. If things went well, they would be married, might even have a baby; she still had a few years left.

Like a symbol of her new life, the bulbs Mary had planted in the cold hard earth of autumn sprang up around her house, a low fence of brilliant color, the very week Will came home.

Will brought a new girlfriend with him, a young Korean woman named Jian. Mary liked her. The sound of her laughter rang like a clear bell. And her skin was the most perfect Mary had ever seen. Whereas many people looked like their features had formed first and their skin fitted over it later, too much in some spots, concealing grit in others, sometimes crinkled or bunched, like a mediocre job of wallpapering, Jian's skin looked like it had settled first, a perfectly smooth blanket beneath which her features had gently pushed into being, clean cuts made for her eyes. Beside her, Will looked handsome, his square face strong. When he lifted his brow in question his forehead wrinkled into three perfectly straight lines, like horizontal pinstripes. Mary could hardly call forth the surly runt the policeman had brought home so long ago. And—wondrously, miraculously—gone were any traces of their sibling rivalry.

The first night of Will's arrival, they all went to Mary's father's house for Passover. Mary was proud as Will read his portion from the Haggadah, her father beaming, finally able to relive the holidays of his childhood without offending his beloved wife. Mary tried to imagine all their ancestors gathered around the table—Mary's mother's Irish Catholic mother, Jian's Asian parents, all the Jewish ghosts of her father's and Sam's parents—shocked at such an assemblage.

Three nights later, she and Sam, and Will and Jian, had Easter dinner at Mary's house. As the dusk took over the house, Mary set the table with her mother's favorite pale pink dishes with mock gold edges. Though she knew they were tacky, Mary loved each plate, the memories they summoned of her mother. When she called everyone to the table, she didn't light the candles immediately. She wanted to admire the beauty of her family in the rose-tinted light of the setting sun. Will and Jian took seats on one side, across from the places set for Mary and Sam. Mary placed the duck, perfectly browned, in the center of the table.

"Ma?" asked Will. "Jian and I still have a couple days before we have to get back and we were wondering, could you recommend someplace we could go for a couple days, just a little overnight trip? I thought about taking the train up to Chicago, but we really aren't crazy about cities."

Mary's heart swelled with pride. She loved it when Will asked her opinion. The perfect television family. She pulled a battered book of matches from her pocket.

"Let me think a minute," she said. She struck the first match and brought the flame to the wicks of the two long-stemmed candles, cupping the flickering lights from behind with her hand, then took her place. In the candlelight, she studied Will's and Jian's expectant faces. She imagined what Jian's face would look like superimposed over Will's. She thought she glimpsed her grandchild.

"Well, maybe if you had a car . . ." Her words were interrupted by the doorbell chimes. "Now who could that be on Easter? Daddy said he was just going to stay home."

"Go ahead, I'll get it," said Sam, placing his napkin on his seat as he pushed back his chair.

"Maybe you could go down to Kentucky; there are some pretty places not too far. I might have a few brochures we could look at after dinner. Maybe we could go with you? Oh . . ." The perfect mom, she realized her mistake immediately. "No, of course, you want to be alone. But you can take my car."

She could hear voices, Sam talking.

"Do you think we should cut this?" asked Will, indicating the duck with a nod of his head.

"I don't know," said Mary, glancing toward the front hall. "I don't know who could be taking so much time. Sam is too polite. He should just tell whoever it is that we're eating. If he's not back in a minute . . ."

"Mary," Sam called from the front door. His voice cracked. "*Mary*."

She put her napkin on the table and rose, perplexed at the urgency in Sam's tone. As she walked to the front hall, she heard Will's and Jian's chair legs scraping: they were rising to follow her. Sam was standing with the front door open to a man, silhouetted against the rosy sunset off her front porch, all his features lost in dark shadow. Mary looked at Sam inquisitively. His intense eyes rueful, Sam looked away. Mary clicked on the hall light, exposing the man's face—a stranger, but a familiar stranger, becoming more familiar as she stared, Will's square face, older, haggard, minus Mary's cheekbones; now Billy's face, aged, his distrustful eyes peeking out from beneath the worn skin of someone else. Mary gasped. All her lives—imagined and real, past and future—seemed to unite in her hall like a dozen lost souls, vessels for wasted dreams.

"Mary," said the man. "I thought that since it was Easter, he might be here, willing to listen . . ."

In the driveway, beyond the porch, Mary saw the hulk of a big old car, battered and well traveled, waiting.

Mary spread her arms and parted her lips in an effort to speak, but no words came out. As if it came from a great distance, she heard Will's voice behind her. "Ma?"

Aunts

In the window, her hair gleamed, as shiny as black patent leather, the flank of a freshly bathed Labrador, even a flapping crow's wing: black and glossy. Lisa bucked her head up and down. Ripple. Ripple. She was dressed entirely in black—black stockings, thin black skirt and sweater, black velvet bow in her hair. Her reflection was black on black glass, a shroud for the train station beyond. Only her face was pale. She knew that to look at her, no one would guess it was the middle of summer. Ripple. Ripple.

"Please stop banging your head. We're going to have to get off in a second," said her mother. She was a difficult woman to heed, her very features being a distraction. The dip between the peaks of her upper lip was so extended that the lip looked like a miniature suspension bridge, a tiny Golden Gate.

"Lisa, listen to us. We're trying to talk to you," said her father.

Ripple. Ripple. Lisa drove her tongue into the sweet wad lodged against the ceiling of her mouth, and blew. Pump. Pump. A pink bubble, a global network of veins, like a pale heart faintly throbbing, grew from her puckered lips. Pink on black.

"Lisa, stop that! Listen to us!"

Crack! The bubble burst, leaving a film, tighter than skin, around her mouth.

"I am listening," she said, rolling her eyes in her parents' direction. She scraped her sticky lips with her teeth.

"Good, honey. Now—above everything else—we want you to know that we love you and we're doing this for your own good."

The Golden Gate moved up and down, making way for minuscule ships. "You're a smart girl, but you're just not thinking clearly right now. You need to get away from, ahhh . . . him."

I know. I know. Thank you, mother.

"The hell I do," she bucked her head back and forth. Ripple. Ripple.

"Lisa! Don't you dare talk to your mother that way!" said her father. The vein that forked through the center of his forehead was pulsating, like a flash of lightning. "And you'd better remember that your aunts are getting old. If I hear that you've used your bad mouth there, you'll be sorry."

I wouldn't talk to them that way. I don't even want to talk that way to you.

"I'm already sorry—sorry you're my parents."

Her father drew back. At first she thought it was to strike her, then she realized that he was the one who looked as if he'd been struck.

"We know you don't mean that—you're just upset now," said her mother; her father had already started down the aisle. "We have to get off now, but we'll call you in a few days."

What? No kiss good-bye? Lisa, too, felt as if she'd been hit.

She put her face to the window, her forehead pressing against the cool glass, and waited. There they were, emerging three cars down: her father looked wilted, a Popsicle-stick man in his huge gray suit, her mother talking and gesturing. Not even a backward glance. Lisa leaned back into her seat. An entire train ride to dream. Trains were best for that, always in motion, pulling her in and out of sleep. All the way from Michigan to Chicago to Springfield, she could dream. The object of her dreams was harmless at a distance. She closed her eyes and brought him to her, her favorite image: Ricky leaning against the brick wall of the Stop-N-Shop, taking slow drags from his Winston, his forehead folded into parallel lines as straight and even as the pale blue lines on her notebook paper, one of his bowlegs bent in an ostrich stance so that the sole of his shoe was wedged against the wall, as he waited for her after school. Then she recalled her mother's words, "Those bowlegs—what a shame. He must have had rickets when he was young." It was like her mother to destroy an image in such a fashion, make a distinction into a disease. Lisa shook her head in an attempt to summon a different image, a gesture she did again and again as the train sped to Chicago, and then over the flat ground of central Illinois.

"Do you want me to spray the plants along this wall, Aunt Val?"

"Well, I don't know that those need to be done again, Lisa," said Aunt Val. "Why don't you grab a bunch of those old pots, take them out back, and splinter them with the mallet. We could use some more clay for drainage."

Lisa took an armload of pots, along with a brown grocery bag and the mallet, out to the courtyard—a circle of hard dirt, adjacent to the door, flanked by two wrought-iron benches. Placing the pots in a line, mouths down, she was slow and deliberate in her work. She didn't want to dream in the daylight or when either of her aunts was around. Dreams were for laziness, drifting in and out of sleep, for solitude. She felt *clean*, squatting on the swept earth, squinting, the warmth of the late afternoon sun spreading across her face. She didn't want to think of anyone or anyplace except where she was at that moment. She tapped the mallet against the first pot in the line, then watched the crack eat through the surface.

The screen door opened behind her.

"Lisa?" Aunt Val asked as she moved around Lisa and took a seat on one of the wrought-iron benches. "There's something I need to talk to you about. I wasn't sure whether or not I should. But you seem so grown-up."

Oh no, not you too. Please don't let it be about Ricky.

Aunt Val was a heavy woman, her thighs, like thick batter poured into a bowl, spread to cover more than half of the bench, which should have seated three. She wore pink shorts and a sleeveless white blouse printed with tiny flowerpots containing tiny pink geraniums.

"It's about Cora May."

"Aunt Cora?"

Aunt Val sighed, a long, drawn-out sigh. Then she shook her head as if to say "Poor Cora May, poor, *poor* Cora May."

"She's not sick, is she?" *About Ricky! How could I have been so self-absorbed?*

"No, not sick. I wish it were that simple," said Aunt Val. "You know why Cora May lives with me, don't you?"

"Because you're sisters. Because you like to live together?"

Lisa eased herself backwards from her squatting position to sitting. Her thighs were getting sore and she knew that when Aunt Val wanted, she could be prolix. If Aunt Cora wasn't sick and the talk wasn't about Ricky, Lisa decided she might as well relax and let Aunt Val reveal information at her own pace.

"Well, yes, yes, we're sisters, that's part of it." Aunt Val released another chest-heaving sigh. "The other reason is that long ago she lost everything she ever owned and now has no place else to go. When our father—your grandfather—died, he gave each of us— Cora, me, and your father—a little money. No fortune, mind you. But enough to last a while if we were careful. Your father, well, he was the baby of the family; he used his for college and his honeymoon. That's all right, considering he was young."

A honeymoon? There were no photographs—where on earth would they go by themselves? Lisa tried to imagine her mother and father, young and alone, leaning over a railing, the roar of Niagara Falls beneath them.

"But Cora and me, well, that's quite a different story. We were older, already had children. Cora May's Michael—and you know what a bum he turned out to be, don't ever name a boy Michael— was almost fifteen I think. That would make my Ilene about ten. So we should have been a little more careful with our money. *I* was. I mean I started this florist business, bought out this place right next to the house—used to be a shoe repair—so I could still be close to home and watch Ilene. I have three gals working for me right now, would be four if you hadn't come for the summer—not that you're not working, but you know what I mean. I don't even need Arthur's Social Security except for pocket money. But Cora May's a different story."

Aunt Val looked up at the sky and sighed, her eyes distant as if she'd forgotten there was a real person listening to her monologue.

"Poor dear. She gave most of her money to her husband, Clyde. And if you think Michael's bad, well, he's just a watered-down version of Clyde. Clyde tried every which way to make that money grow, but, of course, he couldn't since he wasn't willing to put any elbow grease into it, just wanted to invest in hair-brained schemes. And, then, when he'd spent the last of it, he just up and takes off. Just leaves the house one day, then a month later sends a postcard from Palm Springs saying he's a doorman at some fancy hotel out there. Can you imagine?"

Aunt Val was looking at Lisa again, the line of her mouth terse.

"You mean they got divorced?"

"Oh, heavens, no. Something like divorce would have been too simple for the two of them. Cora May just goes on with her life like not a thing has happened, like Clyde is away on a business trip or something. Every eight or nine months he breezes into town and she brings him to family functions, *even holds his hand*, like they're a couple of newlyweds with nothing out of the ordinary wrong."

"Didn't anyone say anything to her?" Lisa shifted into a cross-legged position, and began drawing in the dirt with the tip of a large shard of the broken pot.

"We tried, Lord, we all tried, but Cora May wouldn't hear a bad word about him, and then he stopped coming back, so we just gave up—didn't seem any reason to harp on it. But that brings me around to what I want to tell you about. He's back."

Back from the dead?

"I thought Uncle Clyde was dead."

"Who ever told you that?"

"No one; I just assumed that since he was never here when we came for Easters or Thanksgivings and was never mentioned . . ."

"Well, I suppose that's natural. Though sometimes I do have to wonder about your father, what does get said in your house . . . Well, that's beside the point I guess. The point is that, unfortunately, Clyde is very much alive. I saw him yesterday at Walt's Pharmacy— he looked me right in the eye, then turned and was out the door. Of course, what could he say? 'Sorry I'm a low-down bum and I deserted your sister'? If he has even a lick of pride, he must have been embarrassed to see me. How he could even look me in the eye I don't know."

Aunt Val shook her head.

"But no matter. What we have to do now is keep it from Cora May. If a man calls, tell him she's not home—and she probably won't be if the library keeps her hours up. Don't ask for a message. And if Cora May brings him up—not that I think she would, it's been years since she's talked about him—change the subject. And, most important, if a man should come by, a tall man, about sixty-five with dark hair—he must dye it—gray only at the tips, and asks for Cora May, don't get her. Come get me instead."

What did Aunt Val think?—they were going to run off, a couple of old people who were already married?

"All right, Aunt Val, if you think it's best for Aunt Cora. But what possible harm could he do her now?"

Aunt Val looked at her as if she had said something incredible. Then she sighed, as if the real reason was too complex for Lisa to understand, and, pushing herself up from the bench, said, "You'd have to know Clyde and the type of relationship they had." Aunt Val paused, then added, "What with the problems you had earlier this summer, I thought you might understand."

"Uh-huh," said Lisa, smiling what her father had deemed her smug smile—not that she'd even obliged him with one of those for a while. To think that Aunt Val would compare Clyde to Ricky! *Clyde,* a man who, for most purposes, hadn't existed for probably twenty years. Still, Lisa felt a fabric that had once been whole inside her begin to fray, a gentle tearing. How could she have known Aunt Cora for seventeen years and never wondered what had happened to her husband? Lisa imagined Aunt Cora's face, older than Aunt Val's, but soft and unwrinkled, clear like a translucent watermark on Lisa's mother's expensive stationery, Cora's hair, a blend of red and silver swept back and up into a knot on the top of her head. Her eyes were as blue as the center of a candle's flame. And she was kind, sweet even. Aunt Cora didn't talk to Lisa as much as Aunt Val did, yet when she did she was nice.

But she was old. Old and fat.

Returning to her work, Lisa systematically struck each pot on its upturned bottom with the mallet, then crushed the pieces into chips. When she was finished, she got the broom from the hook by the back door and swept the line of fragments into the paper bag.

"I'm all done, Aunt Val," she called, carrying the bag into the shop. "Is there anything else you want me to do? It's almost four."

"No, I don't suppose so. It doesn't look like we're going to have much more business today. You might as well take off. I'll be home around five to start dinner—of course, if you want to husk the corn it's sitting right by the back door of the house."

"Okay, Auntie Val," Lisa said, sticking the bag under the cashier's counter before leaving.

She walked across the patch of grass that separated the florist shop from Aunt Val's house. Lisa had always loved the little fieldstone house, particularly the front door; placed right next to the chimney, the door was curved across the top so that the bricks set in its frame radiated outward like short beams thrown by a child's rendition of a setting sun; in the center of the door's upper half, a little round porthole, partially obscured by strands of clinging ivy, served as a window. The combination of the chimney and the door had always made Lisa think of cottages in fairy tales. Even though she had cried and carried on about spending the remainder of her summer here, secretly she had been glad. But now, as she looked at the house, she was sorry that she couldn't keep the door in her memory, a place where the house would always look enchanted.

Before Lisa reached the front porch, she noticed that the flag was up on the mailbox, so, pivoting on one foot, she veered toward the driveway. The mailbox, painted by Aunt Cora with bluebirds and twisting vines, had also been special, but now the illustration was so worn and dust-covered that Lisa could see it only by reconstructing the picture in her mind's eye.

When Lisa reached the box, she pulled down the tin flap to reveal a stack of mail.

Right on top was a letter. She could not mistake the small deeply pressed handwriting. Ricky. A letter from Ricky. How had he found her? She felt a quickening in her chest.

She took the letter, closing the flap and leaving the small flag erect, then, almost stumbling, she moved toward the road. To the right was town, and, beyond it, Springfield. She could go to Walt's Pharmacy and drink a root beer float while she read the letter. To the left, the landscape gradually became more rural until there was nothing but a lake of cornfields, broken by the rising crescent of an occasional house or barn.

Without knowing why, she chose the left.

Numbly, her legs moved without her initiative. She went past the Sayers' house with its huge porch framed by intricate wrought-iron railings—what her mother called "architecturally out-of-place, looking like they belonged on a postcard from New Orleans"—past the feed store, two more houses, a dog kennel where angry German shepherds barked at her from their runs, until she was surrounded by corn walls. The flatness seemed unreal to her. How could there be no hills, no undulations? She walked until she came to a space between corn rows that seemed wider than the other openings; she turned and entered as if she were entering a hallway. The corn stretched almost to her shoulders. A few steps inside, just as the road vanished behind

AUNTS

91

her, she reached an unexpected bower, a patch of hard ground where corn either hadn't been planted or had simply failed to grow, and sat down. How could the earth be so level and powdery, as if it were a floor in a building rather than dirt?

She looked at the envelope she'd been carrying, pinched tightly between her thumb and forefinger. Pressed neatly in the return address corner was one word: "outcast." She sighed and ripped the end of the envelope open.

Ricky's letter was less than a page long. Running her hand along the back of the page she could feel his words, pushed beyond the surface by his grip on the pencil:

Dearest Lisa,
I love you. Your brother told me where you are. I love you. As soon as I get paid I'm copping a train for Springfield. I love you. It will get in at 12:30 on Friday night. I love you. You'll need to meet me at the station since I don't know how to get to your aunt's. I love you.

Lisa fell back on the dirt, her hair fanning out beneath her. She closed her eyes and opened them again, bringing the letter an inch away from her face:

We can go anywhere from Springfield and never come back. I love you. We'll always be together forever. I love you.
Ricky (I love you)

She shook her head as if to resist a vision. Tonight. Friday was tonight. The leaves of the cornstalks rustled above her head; beside her, millions of leafy stalks, dancing, brushing against one another in the warm breeze. She shook her head faster. Ripple. Ripple. Her head's movement caused some of the dirt to rise and settle on her face. She felt as if she were in a cloud hovering a fraction of an inch above the ground. She could imagine the smell of Ricky's skin, obscured by a cheap aftershave so powerful and intoxicating that even a whiff of it on a passerby made her knees feel boneless. Love. She had wrapped her arms around him, swearing "I'll never leave you," knowing, as she stared blankly ahead, that her words were untrue. Never. She winced. They had driven for days, eating little and drinking nothing but the wine they had taken from her parents' house. Since they'd had no corkscrew, he had shown her how to drink by breaking the bottle's neck against a curb—he was a practiced hand—then sifting the wine through his T-shirt directly to her mouth so that the glass splinters were caught in the fabric. Everything was a dream, no more real than it was now, images blurred by wine, the spin of the tires against melting tar, the passing of scenery, and hot air streaming in the car window, until they'd been caught.

The breeze picked up, making the rustle of cornstalks grow louder, more persistent, like the rubbing together of dry palms. The ground seemed to fade away beneath her so that she was caught in her cloud, the dome of a rising mushroom cloud, a billowy bed, aware of nothing but the stirring around her, the swish of leaves, the softness against her cheeks, her bare arms and legs. The mushroom was ascending, pushing her toward the blue diamond above her head.

She opened her eyes. How long had she been there? She jumped up and ran toward the road, hoping she hadn't missed dinner. Yet somehow she knew that it was one of those moments—like at home when she woke in a panic, sure she'd missed school, to find that it was early evening—when as deep as her unconsciousness had been, only a short time had passed. Maybe there would still be time to husk the corn.

When she reached her aunts' house, Lisa was surprised to see a blue car in the driveway. They seldom had visitors. *Ricky?* No. He was still at work. It couldn't be Ricky. Besides he didn't have a blue car and his letter had said the train. Still, she would enter by the rear door. If someone was in the living room with her aunts, she could see him from the kitchen before having a confrontation.

She peeked around the corner of the house.

There was a man standing on the porch. He was old, with dark hair combed away from his face so that it ran down to meet at the nape of his neck in a burst of frothy gray curls, a waterfall.

"Hello," said Lisa. "May I help you?"

"Hello," said the man, turning, showing himself to have a youthful grin. The way streamers shot from the corners of his eyes made him—for an old man—almost handsome. "You must be Lisa."

"Yes," she said. "Who are you?"

"My name's Clyde. I'm waiting for your aunt, Cora May."

So it was him, Clyde, the scoundrel. She was supposed to do something if he came by—what was it? Tell Aunt Val?

Just then, the screen door opened and Aunt Cora emerged.

"Oh, hello, Lisa," said Aunt Cora, nervously glancing from the man to Lisa and back again. "I see you've met my friend, Clyde. He was just on his way." She shot a beseeching look at Clyde.

"Yes. Yes," he said. That dashing smile once more. "It was delightful to meet you, Lisa."

"Nice to meet you, too."

With what seemed like just a few long strides, he reached the driveway. Both Lisa and her aunt were silent while they watched him duck into the front seat, then glide down to the road, his neck twisted so that he could see out the rear window.

"Lisa, where have you been? I was worried. Val told me you'd be here husking corn, when I got home."

"Where is Aunt Val?"

Clyde's car disappeared around the bend in the road.

"In town picking up a few things. But she should be back soon, it's almost five-thirty." Aunt Cora paused as if she were deciding whether or not to say more, then gestured toward two lawn chairs placed beneath a cluster of lilac bushes in the yard's farthest corner. "Why don't we sit over there and husk the corn together?"

"Sure, Aunt Cora," said Lisa, grabbing the bag and moving with her aunt to the chairs, turned to catch the setting sun. "How was the library today?"

"Oh, very nice, thank you. I got to do the children's story hour, which is always fun. Usually they have the younger gals do that—and I can't say I blame them—but I certainly enjoy it when I get my chance."

They both returned to silence, quietly stripping the corn. There was a tension, a need on both their parts to say something about Clyde. But Lisa felt too drained, her nap in the cornfield having exhausted her—perhaps it was the sun.

"Lisa?"

"Yes, Aunt Cora?"

"There's a favor I need to ask you."

"Uh-huh?"

"Well, it's about Clyde. I would appreciate it—I mean I think it's best that we not mention Clyde's visit to Val. For some reason, she's taken a dislike to him."

Lisa looked into Aunt Cora's face. There was a trick Lisa had recently discovered for seeing people more clearly. She concentrated on their faces, and pretended she was peering into a mirror, convincing herself she was seeing her own reflection. It was surprising how much more attractive this made people appear. In Cora's case, the result was stunning. She was beautiful. As if a young girl's face were trapped in the wall of flesh. How terrible it must be to have others view you as an old person when you were aware of how you really looked.

"Of course, Aunt Cora. But I think I should tell you, I know Clyde's your husband."

"I'm sorry I lied." Her voice was soft and quiet. "I just didn't want to worry you. I had no idea you knew about him."

"What? Not know my own uncle? But don't *you* worry about it. I just didn't want you to have to pretend."

"Thank you."

Lisa laid a clean ear on her lap, picking away a strand of corn silk, then pulled another ear from the bag.

"How many more should we do?"

"Oh, at least four. With enough, we can practically make a meal out of this corn," said Aunt Cora. She shifted in her chair. When she spoke again, her tone had also shifted. "Lisa, I still think it's best that we don't mention anything about Clyde to Val. It would upset her to know I'm seeing him. I almost . . . well, I probably shouldn't say this . . . but I almost think Val is jealous of my relationship with Clyde. Her and Arthur never did get along too well."

Lisa looked at Aunt Cora. She was an old woman again. Did she even know what she was saying? Lisa wasn't sure whether to feel embarrassed or sad. Jealous of being deserted?

"Aunt Cora, are you sure you have that right? I thought Aunt Val and Arthur were very happy?"

"Oh, yes, I know that's what Val says. And they did get along; Arthur was a fair provider." Aunt Cora smiled a small tight smile. "Yet there was never really any . . . how should I say it? Never really any spark there," she sighed. "But with Clyde. Lord! It still makes me swoon just to hear his voice on the phone!"

An old man's voice? Was it possible he still sounded young to her?

"How long has he been back?"

"This time? Oh, 'round about six years."

"Six years! Aunt Cora! And he just waltzes up here?"

"Oh, heavens, no," Cora chuckled. "I'm sorry. I didn't mean to laugh. But it *is* funny, your thinking he's been in town six years without bothering to call. I see him once or twice a week. He hasn't been right in town. He's been working in Springfield, has a little apartment there that I helped him fix up."

"But why, Auntie Cora? Why do you put up with it?"

"Put up with what? He's just not quite ready to get back together full-time. Probably never should have tried to set up house in the first place. And, to be truthful, he's never been too solid financially, so it's best all around that I stay on with Val. Can you imagine how lonesome she'd get? So he comes to the library on his day off for lunch or I say I'm going out with some of the gals from the library or working late, and we get ourselves a night out. That's one of the reasons I've never given in to Val's wanting me to work at her shop. I'd lose my independence. Besides, I know that after a while I'd just crowd him."

"Independence? I thought you needed to live with Aunt Val?"

"Oh, she likes to think that. And if it makes her feel good, what's the harm?"

"But what about tonight? What if she caught him? What was he even doing here?"

"He does stop by here occasionally. I've asked him not to, but sometimes he can't help himself, he has to see me. And, well, lately he's wanted to stop all the sneaking around. He says Val saw him at the drugstore so the jig's up, and we might as well come out in the open." Cora shrugged and placed an ear of corn in the bag. "I think we've got enough."

"What do *you* want, Aunt Cora?"

"Oh, about telling Val? I don't want to hurt Clyde's feelings but I believe that Val has such a low opinion of him that even if she did recognize him in the drugstore, she wouldn't necessarily guess that the jig is up, so to speak. She would just think he was passing through town. So I think it's best that we keep things as they are."

They heard the spray of gravel, like rain stinging a roof, as Val's car turned up the drive.

They had string beans, a little fried chicken, and lots of corn for dinner. Lisa knew why the "corn-fed" folks in southern Illinois were often chunky. Even she was beginning to put on weight. She felt under the table for the sway of her stomach. Would Ricky notice? Ricky! He would be in Springfield in less than four hours and she still hadn't made up her mind. She traced the outline of a pear on the oilcloth table covering and tried to concentrate on what Aunt Val was saying.

"I think you best just plan on staying here over Labor Day, what with Michael starting a new job. A DJ! Lord have mercy! No offense, Cora May, but it is a little difficult to believe that someone is actually going to pay him just to talk. Though I will admit he could talk forever and never say a word."

Aunt Cora just smiled her secretive little smile.

"Anyway, with him just moving into a new place—you better hope he never has children, they'd never be able to remember their address—you don't want to burden him with one more thing to think about."

The phone rang.

Lisa felt her back stiffen.

"I'll get it," said Aunt Val, shoving herself up from the table. She walked to where the phone hung near the back door and lifted the receiver on the third ring.

"Hello? Hello? Anyone there?—well, will you beat that? Whoever it was hung up when they heard my voice."

Lisa stared at her Aunt Val. From the corner of her eye, she could see that Cora May was also staring.

Cora May blinked. "Oh, probably just a wrong number." She dusted her skirt with her open hands. "You know how people are these days, so busy that there's no time to explain."

"If you two don't mind," said Lisa, "I think I'll go to bed. I don't feel very well."

"Is there something I can get you, honey?"

"No. My stomach is just a little upset. I think if I go lie down I'll be okay."

"Well, if you're sure."

"Uh-huh. I might even get back up in an hour or two."

She didn't remove her clothing, instead choosing to rest on top of the chenille bedspread, her hands palms down, sweeping back and forth over the puffy balls, in lines like rows of miniature cabbages.

She heard doors open and close. She heard Sailor, the cat, called inside. The distant mumble of the television came on for an hour or so. As the light faded, her room growing gray, she heard the bathwater run and drain. They were preparing for bed. She ignored a faint knock on her door, and closed her eyes when the door opened a crack. She drifted in and out of sleep, as if she were riding a long train. If she was going to leave, she would have to go soon.

She pictured Ricky's face. The first time she had looked at him pretending she was peering into a mirror she had surprised herself by thinking, "So, this is what it's like to be desperate." Until that moment she had never thought of him as desperate. She had known he wasn't normal. Not completely. As her father had said, "Why would any twenty-three year old even want to run off with a high school girl? He's just lucky we didn't have him thrown in jail." But Ricky wasn't crazy, just sad. She saw herself wide eyed, indifferent, her arms wrapped around his shoulders, saying, "I'll never leave you." She plucked a thread from a miniature cabbage head and winced.

Leaving her aunts' home was more complicated than leaving her parents'. Her aunts would blame themselves. They would worry. She would never be able to face them again.

But Ricky. She imagined Ricky all alone, stepping from the train in Springfield on his jaunty bowlegs, his brow wrinkled, a cigarette dangling from his lips as he looked for her. He would think her absence was due to fear, not the result of her not loving him enough to endlessly wander, never knowing where they would settle. She remembered a place where they had stayed, an apartment belonging to a friend of Ricky's. Located above a Laundromat, it was sadly decorated with lava lamps and fishnets draped from corners, as if the friend envisioned himself to be a swinging single. They had stayed there only two days, but the heat rising from the dryers below made Lisa so languid that she felt she would never rise from the mattress that she and Ricky shared, instead melting deeper and deeper into the damp fabric.

She glanced at the luminous arms of her alarm clock and leaped off the bed. It was nearly one o'clock! How had she fallen asleep? What had caused her to wake up? A noise in the yard, a rustling of shrubbery. Ricky was in the yard! How had he found her aunts' house?

Lisa hurried to the tall oak chiffonier and yanked open one of the top drawers. A week's worth of underwear, two T-shirts, two pairs of shorts, and a sundress. She wouldn't need more. She shook her pillow out of its case and stuffed the clothing inside, knotting the top. All she needed to do was slide the screen up and fall to the ground. Ricky would be waiting. She pushed the notches toward the center and moved the screen upwards. One leg at a time, she swung over the ledge, her feet dangling. It was like sitting on the edge of a swimming pool; she pushed away with her hands, holding tightly to the pillowcase, and landed catlike in the thick grass. Something moved. She heard a whisper. Ricky was calling her. She crept quietly in the direction of the noise, the moon, big and silver as a pie tin in the sky, lighting her way. The noise had come from the cluster of lilac bushes. She swept aside a drooping branch expecting to see Ricky, but was so startled by what she encountered that she dropped her pillow sack. The grass seemed to harden around her feet, trapping her. There in a wash of silver light, wearing a thin lavender nightgown, was her aunt Cora May, caught in the arms of her husband, her breath only inches from Lisa but her eyes were closed so tight in rapture that she was aware of nothing but Clyde. Her hair, worn down, fell over her left shoulder and the side of her face so that only a strip of skin, freckled and girlish, next to Clyde's waterfall of hair, was visible. As soon as the grass felt soft on her heels, Lisa moved quietly backwards, not wanting to disturb them. There was no need to stoop to retrieve her pillowcase. She knew in one fleeting moment when, try as she might, she could not make herself believe her aunt's face was her own, thrown back from a mirror, that she would be going nowhere.

Maps

*I*t happens the way it always happens when we visit my husband's family: quickly, in unison, like crows drawn to seed, they turn to discussing directions, the routes they take to different places, to this gathering in particular. They are all men, my husband's family. There is my father-in-law, Harry, and his three grown sons. (The mother left when the youngest was a newborn, and died in a car accident just days later. She is never mentioned.) They argue about which way is quickest and who gave the best directions. It's as if they know nothing but routes.

I tease my husband, John, a lot about this. "Tease" might be too mild a word. After the last visit, I was actually upset. Clutching the car door handle, my voice rising, I asked, "Why don't you guys ever *talk*?" John was staring straight ahead, over the steering wheel. We were driving west on I-94, a flat road without barriers on either side so that the snow swept across it in great sheets, drifting on the other side in ghostly dunes. Instead of acquiescing to his silence, I persisted. "Don't you want to know more than how they got there? Or the best way to the mall? Aren't you curious about their lives? Their jobs? Whether they're seeing anyone now?" (John is the only one with a wife, though I assume the others must, from time to time, have lovers.) John didn't really answer, he just shrugged, "That's the way we are."

At that point, I recall, the snow rose, enormous white gusts around the car, like dancing spirits ascending from the earth.

"Maybe we should turn back," I said.

"No," said John. "I know this road like the back of my hand." I sighed.

But tonight, during this visit, I'm not annoyed, simply resigned. I feel a cold coming on, my muscles ache, and my skin feels feverish. I have a dull headache. Usually I like to nurture these womenless men: At my house I bring them tea and homemade soup, at theirs, chips and beer. The generous side of my nature wants to soften their lives, show them the pleasure of a woman's touch, while my manipulative side wants to say, "Look, see what you're missing. See how good John has it." (Though they'd never admit it, they don't fully approve of me. I can sense it. They're bothered by the fact that I was married before and have a son from that marriage. Losing a mother so young—even the way they did—has given them unreal expectations of women, idealistic notions.) Yet, tonight I am too weak to perform domestic tasks. I simply want to rest sideways on the sofa, feel my body sink into the cushions, mold with them, my warm cheek resting against the fabric.

Already the men have been talking about roads for almost an hour. In David's La-Z-Boy recliner, Harry has given a lively account of how he came to arrive. David, the oldest son, bereft of any recent travel due to the fact that we're at his condominium, is just finishing explaining the new route he has to take to work due to construction under way on his former route.

"You should have told me that they have a detour on Harrison," interrupts Kansas, the youngest brother. He is the only one with an unusual name. "David" and "John" were obviously the collaborative choice of both parents: sensible, solid names. But Harry must have been left on his own to name Kansas and, in a rush of grief and senti-mentality, settled on the birth state of his dead wife. I wonder if he's ever regretted it, and if the name is the reason Kansas seems to carry himself differently from his brothers, why he seems self-conscious and watchful, never enters a door head-on, instead slipping through sideways, or if it's because he has lived his entire life motherless? It's hard to know. He is only twenty-five, seven years younger than John; he has a lot of changing to do.

"Hell. I told you not to take Harrison," says David. "I said to come straight off 94."

"But you didn't say there was a detour."

"Maybe not, maybe I forgot, but straight off is the fastest way anyhow."

"You've gotta be kiddin'!"

I close my eyes, lulled by aches and fever, but I feel John, beside me, shift in uneasiness.

"Oh, what does it matter?" says John, his voice cracking. "We're all here, aren't we?"

There is a silence. I open my eyes. They are watery, another symptom of my cold spreading. Even the light from David's one small lamp hurts. Harry is still in the recliner. David is sitting on a chrome chair with a plastic seat he's carried out from his kitchen, while Kansas, still the child of the family, sits cross-legged on the floor. Through the haze of my illness, there is a surreal quality to the group. Even though they're all related, they appear as different from one another as illustrations rendered by artists with wholly different styles.

John leans forward, resting a strong forearm on his knee, poised to make his pitch. I see he has been waiting for this moment. He doesn't realize I'm becoming sick. He thinks that I'm quiet, drifting away to my thoughts, because of boredom, perhaps even disgust, with the conversation. He is doing this for me.

"I mean, why don't we really *talk*?"

"I thought that's what we were doing," says Harry. Even with my watery eyes, I can see the way his face sags. I envision, as I did when I first met him, how he must have looked when he arrived at the hospital to claim his wife and newborn son, and learned that his wife was gone. I imagine him carrying the infant from the hospital. And for the first time, I wonder if he's ever traced the route his wife and her lover took from the hospital to their fatal crash.

"I mean *really* talk." John glances at me for support. I do nothing, neither encourage nor discourage him, but my passiveness makes me feel like more of a traitor than either course of action could. "About our jobs. What we're doing. You know. I mean, Kansas, I don't even know if you have a girlfriend!"

Now the walls, the carpet, the very air seem thicker. Shifting my bulk, I glance at the framed Edward Hopper poster, *Nighthawks*, above Kansas's head, on the wall next to the kitchen door. With my fever and blurred vision, I think I see it the way it's supposed to be seen—all shadows and angles. I remember when David bought it, how he had proudly shown it to me, eagerly awaiting my approval, wanting to know that a woman liked it, even—maybe particularly— a woman he didn't quite approve of. I had thought of all the snobby, condescending remarks I could have made—how I'd always thought of Hopper as more of an illustrator than an artist—but instead I had said, "I like it; it looks great on that wall," and meant what I said.

"Well," Kansas looks down, tugging at a strand from the thick carpet pile, "I am seeing someone, a woman named Sue."

"That's great," says John, beaming, reminiscent of a teacher who has pried the correct answer from an unusually reticent student. Doesn't he realize how unbearable this is?

"Where did you meet her?"

John is more handsome, more sure of himself, than his brothers, but he is generally quiet, thoughtful, which makes it all the more disconcerting seeing him in this role of talk show host. My soul is paradoxically overcome with both pain and love—pain at seeing him so outside himself, and love at knowing he is doing this for me.

John, I want to say, *you don't need to do this.* But still I am frozen, my mouth and body immovable.

"At work," says Kansas. "She's a secretary at the office."

"How old is she?" asks Harry.

"Oh, I don't know," says Kansas, still looking down. "Around thirty."

"You don't know? I dare say you could check it out," says Harry. "Five years older than you—I hope you're not serious."

"That's not such a bad age difference," I say, surprised by the hoarse quality of my voice. I'm even sicker than I had imagined. Everyone looks at me and I realize it's the first time I've spoken since the greetings when we arrived.

"Maybe not, if you don't want kids," says Harry, his voice stern. "Or if you've already got some."

Is this criticism directed at me or at the faceless woman? I'm too sick to analyze Harry's tone. Besides, I'm afraid to answer: I want too vehemently to defend this woman, to make her cause my own. I don't know if my passion is rational or the result of my fever. I don't trust myself, so I remain quiet.

"Lots of women these days have babies in their late thirties, even in their forties," says John.

"Maybe movie stars," says Harry.

Kansas has not moved. In addition to my physical illness, my heart now feels weighted. Kansas is not a bad-looking man. He has a heavy jaw, broad shoulders, and a rare but pleasantly shy smile. The veins on his hands are thick and blue. Perhaps with a mother to praise him, even for only a few years, he would have been handsome.

I sense that John, too, realizes how poorly his attempt at intimacy is going. But once set in motion, he can't stop himself. "What about you, David? You got a girl?"

From schoolteacher to talk show host to cowboy: John is not accustomed to playing so many characters. That is my role, the role of the only women in this odd group. Watching him is like watching a brakeless vehicle traveling downhill, collecting and losing different camouflages as it passes through underbrush.

"Yeah," says David.

"No kidding," says Kansas, looking up, obviously relieved to have the attention directed elsewhere. "Where did you meet her?"

"In the fall, on a trip to see Steve, our last time taking the boat out on Lake Erie for the season. She's Steve's wife's cousin."

"All the way last fall?" asks John. He seems genuinely surprised. "How come this is the first we've heard of her?"

David shrugs.

"Does she live in Ohio?" asks Kansas.

"Uh-huh, outside Akron."

"Wow, how often do you see her?" The "wow" makes Kansas seem even younger than his twenty-five years.

"Every week or two."

"Do you take the turnpike?" asks Harry.

"Of course," says David.

"No, no," says Harry, shaking his head in disgust, his jowls jiggling. Through my fever-induced haze, I see him dig his fingers into the arms of the La-Z-Boy and hoist himself up. "Where's your map? I can show you a way that cuts a half hour off that, easy."

"No," says David. "I checked it out." He is also rising, but not in anger or to argue. The cloud of discomfort is lifting; the father and his sons are again in familiar territory. "The maps are in the kitchen, in the broom closet."

Kansas, too, is standing, brushing off the seat of his pants, following David and Harry into the kitchen.

John whispers in my ear. "Are you okay?"

I nod, my cheek sweeping the fabric, "I'm coming down with something, but I'll be all right. You go, go with them to the kitchen."

He kisses me lightly on the forehead and is gone. I hear someone, probably David, ask, "What about Meg?"

"She's got a bug," John says. "She'd rather just stay on the couch."

Paper rustles. I know it's the map. In my mind's eye, I envision its worn edges, the intricate crisscrossing design of pale blue and red lines. They're spreading the map across the kitchen table, beneath the hanging lamp. I don't need to be there to know; I've seen this ritual dozens of times—the map blanketing a picnic table, a coffee table, the hood of a car, the men gathering, converging, like a flock of crows.

"Want a beer?" David asks. I hear the refrigerator door. "I could reheat this chili or what about some hot dogs?" It is like him to invite everyone and not consider what he will serve beforehand. But I don't have time to ponder this before I am dreaming—if one could call it that. I can still hear the distant murmur of the men's voices, the dream is really a memory, only relayed in the way a dream unfolds, the end being inevitable, expected, yet also a surprise, as if it had neither been planned by me nor actually lived out at an earlier time in my life.

I'm recalling the first time I went out with John. He was the first person I'd gone out with in months. Being a divorced mother was such an odd state that I'd finally decided it was easier simply to be a mother to Ben than try to date like a single woman. But when I met John, he seemed so kind, his invitation so natural, that I had accepted without thinking.

It wasn't until the afternoon of our date that I had begun to have second thoughts. Ben and I were living out in the country, not a bad house, though a bit run-down. Ben's father had stopped paying child support and since I was in graduate school, only working part-time, and only had an occasional check from my parents, I didn't have money to keep the place up. There weren't many other houses around. Behind us was woods, with the railroad track buried deep in its midst. To the left was a marshy pond with floating ice sheets rising like congealed grease to a pot's surface, and a half mile to the right was an electric power plant with six steel structures fenced together like a bank of Eiffel Towers. But none of that was depressing when compared to the place across the street, the Lee house.

In the same way you can't call my dream a dream, you couldn't call the Lee house a house. They had planned to build a four-bedroom ranch but had exhausted their money before they'd completed the foundation, so they had merely finished the basement and front hallway and door (which rose from the foundation like a monstrous periscope emerging from the sea), slapped some tar paper on the hall walls and a roof across the basement, and moved in—all eight of them. "Mole people," I called them to Ben. His eyes would widen, partly I'm sure in fright, partly in fascination, as any child imagining some secret connection between man and beast.

I had stood there that afternoon, at the edge of my yard—wind whistling through the broken picket fence curving along the drive behind me, paint on my own house peeling in flakes as large as autumn leaves—watching the tar paper on the Lee hallway flap in the freezing wind while I waited for Ben's bus. I remembered riding the bus when I was a girl. I had been a townie, had lived only a block from the elementary school in a two-story brick house with a two-car garage. But sometimes I liked to ride home with my friends to see what it was like to travel away from town, over rolling hills to farms or distant developments.

There was one stop on the bus trip that I found particularly intriguing—Gloria Eggsford's house. It was nothing more than a series of chicken coops attached by wire and tar paper hallways. How could anyone live there? She was the only poor girl any of us knew so we all pressed our faces to the windows when the bus halted at her drive. Usually she would just dart into the conglomeration of shacks without glancing back. But sometimes she would fling a mud patty at the departing bus's rear window. Other times she would twirl around, her limp blond hair barely rising to skirt her face, and shout, "Take a picture! It lasts longer!"

Once, in junior high, during the peak of our adolescent cruelty, three of us had sat behind her on the bus, quietly singing, "*Gloria, G-L-O-R-I-A. Gloria. She come up to ma house. She call ma name. She make me feel all right. Gloria. G-L-O . . .*" Before we could finish, she turned on us, brandishing a rat-tailed comb as if it were a knife, and hissed with such hatred that she managed to overcome the banality of the cliché issuing from her lips. "Sticks and stones will break my bones, but names will never hurt me."

How alone she must have felt.

And as I stood there that day recalling Gloria and waiting for Ben's bus so that we could begin waiting for the baby-sitter, then for John,

I felt alone, so alone that I was struck by a terrible thought. What if the children on Ben's bus looked at us the way we'd looked at Gloria? No, no, I told myself, our house was really a house, just a little run-down. I was a single parent in graduate school, temporarily set back, not a member of the chronic poor. But my argument wasn't convincing. By the time Ben's orange bus pulled up to our drive, I was in a panic. My heart swelled with pity as I watched Ben swing down from the bus's high bottom step, one hand grasping the metal side pole while the other clutched his Donald Duck lunch bucket. I couldn't bring myself to look up at the bus windows; rather, I took Ben's hand and said, "Come on, let's get out of this cold."

I decided that I could not have John pick me up at our house. If he saw how poor I was, I would be too vulnerable, not in a sexual sense, but in some other oblique, far more dangerous way.

As soon as I pulled Ben's snowsuit off, I called the baby-sitter and asked if Ben could spend the night at her house. Then I called John and asked him if I could meet him at the restaurant. I told him that it would be easier, that I had some errands I wanted to complete on the way.

As I sit here on the couch, on the periphery of consciousness— half recalling, half dreaming, while I listen to the men talking about alternative routes—I clearly remember the mustard color of the telephone we had in that house in the country, the way the receiver, smeared with fingerprints, looked as I placed it back in the cradle. I would make the most of the evening, I had told myself as I wiped the phone with a damp rag, but I would never see John again.

That night, John and I ate spinach and feta pies at a Greek restaurant, together grew hot from the flaming cheeses being served around us, and laughed and drank wine until very late. But nothing happened to change my resolve.

When I pulled in my driveway at the evening's end, I noticed the gas tank was on empty, but I imagined there would be enough to get me to the corner gas station when it opened in the morning. It was so cold that I pulled as close to the house as possible, yet stood in the drive for a moment to feel the night air, watch my own breath take shape in it, and to sober myself.

As soon as I walked in the front door of the house, I knew something was wrong. I was not struck by the warmth I had expected. In fact there was no change from the outside. I could still see my breath, and the windows, glazed with frost, sparkled from the moonlight shining through. I walked quickly to the kitchen and felt the linoleum crackle beneath my boots. The floor was frozen. I placed my hand by a vent, but felt nothing. I could not remember when they had last come and filled the oil tank in the basement. I knew I had missed a bill, just one; that wouldn't stop them, would it? But before I even had time to consider, I knew it had. Of course, they were a company; they didn't sit around and think, "Well, we'll give her one more chance."

Then the magnitude of the problem struck me. It was two in the morning, ten degrees below freezing; there was no heat in my house, no gas in my car, and to top it off, I was drunk.

Even here on the couch, knowing in one section of my mind what eventually happened, I worry and wonder in all the other sections how I will get out of the predicament. *Call John,* an inner voice of mine says, and I do, reasoning he was the one person I knew who was still awake, and since I was never going to see him again anyway, his reaction didn't matter.

"Sure," he said. "I remember your directions. I'll just siphon some oil from here. See you in about forty minutes. Wrap yourself in a blanket. Don't go to sleep."

I followed his advice, used the heavy quilt from Ben's bed as a shawl, and pulled the wicker rocker up to the front window. I still smoked then, so as I waited I concentrated on the amber glow of my cigarette and on the moonlit Lee house—the solitary door rising from the earth—across the street. Even if the dilapidation of my house was disguised by the darkness, the Lee place would surely reveal the caliber of the neighborhood.

John arrived forty minutes to the second with both oil for the furnace and gas for the car. We stood together on the concrete basement floor while he poured oil in the tank. He didn't mention anything about the house. All he said was "I'm going to stay until the place begins to warm up."

We sat on the couch and talked, about nothing really, until finally I couldn't stand it any longer and blurted out, "Well, what do you think?"

"About what?" he said.

"You know, about where I live."

He looked puzzled, but tried to answer, slowly at first.

"Well, it's not as far out as I thought. It took me almost twenty minutes to siphon the gas and oil and I worried that it would take me another thirty to get here. I almost called to let you know I was going to be longer, then I remembered Stone Creek Road. Do you know it? There's no businesses on it so I guess nobody uses it much anymore. But there's not a single light, and as long as there weren't any trains crossing tonight—I knew that was a risk—I guessed I'd be able to cut five, ten minutes off the trip. . . ." He went on and on, describing a covered bridge he had passed on the way, and a family of rabbits crossing the glittering snow; he never did get to mentioning what he thought of my house, which made it clear he didn't care.

Of course, I did see him again, and again and again. And in the spring without us ever really discussing it, we began to repair the fence together, then to paint the house.

It is at this point in my dream/memory, as I watch our arms go up and down, planting brush strokes, spreading white paint, that the border between sleep and wakefulness fades; I can no longer hear the men's voices and I think that I'm asleep.

The next thing I know John is gently shaking me, kissing my hair. "Come on, babe, I've warmed up the car. It's late, we've got to go." He places his hand on my brow, under my bangs. "You're really hot. I think you have a fever. Here get up, put your coat on."

My skin is burning now, and my throat feels raspy, like every breath draws up glass splinters. Beyond John, I see David holding my coat open. John guides my arms backwards into the waiting sleeves.

"All you've got to do is make it to the car; then you'll be warm again," John says.

"Don't worry. I'm okay," I say.

Despite my raging fever—or maybe because of it—the cold night air feels good. My heart flutters in my chest, no doubt reacting to the sudden contrast. But I feel more alive than I've felt in a long time, perhaps because I feel so much. I want to go home and make love, feel the balm of John's cool chest moving against the skin of my warm breasts. Of all the reasons for lovemaking, to soothe pain seems to be the purest. John helps me into the car, then when he gets in, he pulls me next to him; I realize we will look, in the headlights of oncoming cars, our two heads together, like teenagers in love.

I twist my head around and look out the rear window. Although I know I have neither the energy nor the concentration to endure this for the entire journey, I at least want to try to remember the route we are taking. But before we have even rounded the sycamore grove at the end of David's condominium parking lot, I have lost myself in the sparkling beads of ice bordering the window.

Where You Can't Touch Bottom

*C*rouched on the floor by her bedroom window, Libby watched the glow of her cigarette as she waited. A bead of amber radiated between the white cylinder and the growing band of ash—the only light in the room. She knew she didn't *have* to wait. She didn't have to go with them. She could go back to bed, pretend not to hear them when they appeared beneath her window. She didn't *want* to go with them. She was afraid.

Libby carefully rolled the ash against the windowsill so it separated from the cigarette. A perfect unbroken band of gray and white flakes, still holding the shape of its former self.

"Libby, Libby," a hushed voice rose from below, then a chorus of whispers. "Lib-bee, Lib-bee, Lib-bee."

She crushed the stub out in the well of the sill. Yes. She had to go with them. She had no choice.

"Quiet, I'm coming," Libby called down. She gathered her tennis shoes and tossed them out the window so that they sailed above and beyond the attached garage roof.

"Catch," she called after them.

A seasoned night crawler, Libby slipped deftly over her windowsill onto the garage. The shingles felt gritty under her bare feet. Steadying herself, she walked sideways down the slope to the edge. She sank to her knees, then holding tight to the gutter, pushed away from the roof so that she swung a story above ground. Swinging from her clasped hands, she hesitated. Her hips felt as weighted as a heavy belt, her belly as stretched as Turkish Taffy. The summer before, this part— the dropping—had been no more difficult than climbing over the sill. But now that her breasts and hips had swollen in disproportion to her thin legs and arms, she felt awkward. Adjusting to an adult body, a body that seemed to belong to someone else, restricted the flexibility she had grown to expect. She dreaded the hard drop to earth, her tiny feet having to balance such a grown-up body.

"Let go, Libby, come on!" She recognized her best friend Maudie's voice.

Libby closed her eyes and released her fingers. She felt a rush in her belly, then the solid earth, the sting in her heels. She didn't care; at least she didn't topple. She became aware of the moist grass between her toes, and looked around, just enough moon to make out five or six forms. Someone handed her shoes to her. She sat down to slip them on. The forms towered over her. As soon as her eyes adjusted, the moonlight would be sufficient for her to distinguish faces.

"Hurry," said Maudie. "Your parents' light is still on."

Libby tied quick sloppy bows and stood up.

"Come on," said a raspy male voice that Libby recognized as Casey McIntyre's. He ran across the street. They all followed, across the black asphalt, shining like a river in the moonlight. They ran around the corner, ducking under bushes, into the backyards of Elm Street, to the far back where they formed a running line along the borders of yards. The night air clung, cool and moist, to Libby's forearms. Except for an occasional whisper, only the rustle of cotton summer clothing could be heard as they ran. Libby felt the crotch of the one-piece bathing suit she wore beneath her clothes ride up her crack. She wished she could stop to pull it down. But a pause could be dangerous; someone might see them and call their parents before they reached their destination. They were going to the field far behind the high school to swim in the old water tower standing sentry at the edge of East Hubbard Woods.

When Libby thought of it, her underarms prickled in fear and adrenalin shot from the pit of her stomach like a geyser. The boys had made this excursion before, but not the girls.

"It's easy," Casey had assured them the day before in Hubbard's Drug Store. "Nothing to it. We drop a rope in so if you get cramps or something, you can hang on until you feel better. Besides, someone will stay outside on the scaffolding in case anything goes wrong."

Libby had sipped her cherry phosphate and spun around on her fountain stool.

"So, what if something *does* go wrong?" Susan demanded, hands on her hips. By tacit agreement, she was the leader of the girls, the strongest of them, the prettiest. "Is that somebody going to run all the way back to downtown Hubbard and get an ambulance?"

"Nothing is gonna go that wrong," retorted Casey. "Besides, the rest of us will be right there."

"I don't know," said Susan, shaking her head softly so that the ropes of her lustrous brown hair swung slightly.

Libby also didn't know, but she was too timid to speak up. Lately, their regular weekend nocturnal jaunts seemed to grow progressively less cautious. At first being outside without permission while the rest of the town slept was enough. They simply roamed Hubbard, the small Illinois village where they lived. When Libby grew up and moved away, people would find her allusions to the village where she grew up curious, parochial, sometimes even pretentious given she hadn't lived abroad. But her portrayal was accurate. Too little populated to be incorporated with the township into a city, it really was a village. The core—the town square with a circle of park benches, a flagpole, and an old clock tower—was protected from time and cities, as with obsidian glass, by several layers: first the shops, next the tall white Victorian houses standing deceptively proper inside wrought-iron fences, and finally, the outer shell, sprawling farmland that kept Hubbard safe from the distant city and encroaching suburbs.

Walking through Hubbard late at night, a pack of adolescents, they felt like the only survivors in an abandoned land, as if they had taken possession, or been the only ones spared in a nuclear disaster. Libby liked the feeling of owning, of belonging, so much in fact that sometimes it bothered her in the light of day to see so many people freely roaming their town, *her* town.

But now, claiming the village wasn't enough. They wanted more, particularly the boys. And the more they took, the more Libby felt they were losing. She was having a harder time sustaining mystery in the ordinary, but even more difficulty holding on to what was hers. She wasn't brave like Susan. She couldn't openly protest—not that it would matter. She knew she couldn't yet articulate what she felt, couldn't put it into words.

A few weeks before, Libby and four other girls had walked all the way out to meet the boys at the old cemetery, the one with ancient gravestones with quaint sayings that the elderly women of Hubbard used to make grave rubbings. Some of the stones were so worn that the relief letters appeared to be in the final stages of melting. All the stones—from years of rain and wind—slanted backward, like resistant hairs combed in the wrong direction. While waiting for the boys, Susan, Libby, Maudie, and the other two girls had tiptoed between the huge tombstones, reading the epigraphs to each other by the beam of their single flashlight. They made up stories about the people buried beneath their feet. Libby was filled with a sense of longing and desire for things she would never feel, people she would never know, a pleasant desire, a desire that suggested there was so much to feel, so much she couldn't have that she could go on looking forever. But when the boys arrived, the mood changed. They wanted to play "ghost," running from headstone to headstone. The raucousness would have destroyed the evening were it not for the fact that when the horizon glowed pink, they departed from the boys. In order to be home before their parents awoke, the girls hitched a ride on a milk truck. Many years later, when Libby saw an etching of multiarmed Siva, Hindu god of war and reproduction, she would recall the ride and imagine the truck, all the girls on the running boards, their many pale arms waving against the pastel sky. The etching would help her understand where her process of forever reining in had begun: how even when she became a competent woman, in control, she would sometimes delay understanding the layout of a city in order to preserve the mystery of place, and no matter how many times she made love with the same man she would always return to the study of her hand in his, trace his veins with her index finger, a way to prevent the power of sexual intimacy from obscuring the wonder of first touch. She would remember the water tower and know that it was possible to keep control, yet reach out, without risking the sense of mystery. But that night as she ran, Libby could know nothing of all this. She could only feel dread at the thought of what awaited her, fear of being sealed off inside the enormous drum of the water tower.

Breathless from running, Libby was relieved when they reached the field, leaving the houses behind them, so they could revert to walking. She was almost happy until she saw the water tower looming in the distance. Silhouetted against the sky, the tower rose above the woods on soaring stiltlike legs. On top sat a gigantic ball covered by a peaked roof. It looked like a big-bellied monster wearing a conical Chinese coolie's hat. Libby remembered trolls and giants from childhood reading. Was she really going to climb inside that belly voluntarily? Libby looked at the others. In the open field, the moonlight bathed and elucidated their features. Libby could make out faces: Casey, Randy Foster, Sam Woods, and—Lucy sighed— Dusty Walker.

"Are *we* the only girls?" Libby whispered to Maudie.

Maudie shrugged. "Everyone else chickened out." Libby took a deep breath. She knew the opposite was true. The others had been brave enough to say no. But she couldn't say this to Maudie. Now that they were in, Libby knew she would have to play it the other way, that they were adventurers. But even though Maudie was her best friend, Libby wished that if there had to be only two girls, that Susan was the other girl.

The boys were talking among themselves, laughing and boasting of their feats the last time they'd gone swimming in the tower. How Casey had saved Sam by grabbing his hair when he swallowed a mouthful of filthy water. How Dusty had almost scaled a slimy wall— would have, in fact, if he hadn't been cut by a jutting scrap of metal. How Randy had treaded in place, his hands above his head, singing six rounds of "Yellow Submarine."

Randy flipped on the portable radio he always carried. A static-ridden "Johnny Be Good" blared; the boys whipped out their invisible guitars. It was a phenomenon Libby would notice many times over the next twenty years—most guys her age were never without their invisible guitars. Well into their forties, they packed these instruments; only the frequency in which the air guitars appeared, and the boldness with which they were played, changed.

Casey squatted, closed his eyes, and threw his head back, never losing his grip on the illusory instrument. Everyone laughed. Randy joined Casey in the exaggerated pose, extending his feet out in front of his body in quick jerks so that his knees followed and his belly became a table on which to strum the guitar. They all laughed harder. For a moment Libby forgot the purpose of their mission. She closed her eyes in laughter. The night air hugged her, permeating her clothing, as thick and tangible as cool smoke rising, billowing, enclosing her. She was caught in laughter and freedom and the smell of summer grass. Then she opened her eyes. Dusty was looking at her, his eyes slits. She shuddered and tugged Maudie's sleeve.

"Come on," she whispered. "We better go ahead to undress."

"See you guys at the water tower!" Maudie said, her voice too cheerful, too solicitous, as if she was afraid the boys might not follow.

Had she known she and Maudie would be alone in a group of boys that included Dusty, Libby would have been able to say no without qualms. In the spring she had thought he was her friend. Even though he was going with Susan, the prettiest girl in the high school, Dusty seemed to like to talk to Libby. Sometimes they walked home from school together. She thought he told her things that he never told anyone else. Yes, she was sure, they were friends. So she had taken him to her favorite place, a vast but private stretch of land behind the oldest barn outside Hubbard, the one with the little steeple and the year 1834 stenciled on the roof.

They had walked against the sun. Libby loved the heat spreading across her cheeks, the long yellow grass brushing her bare legs. She felt wonderful, clean and happy. So when Dusty turned to her and said "Can I ask you something?" she had thought it could only be something wonderful. She said yes quickly. He looked her in the face. Libby was surprised by the glassy look in his eyes. His face was red and grimy from the heat, his lips were almost swollen, and a single drop of sweat cut a path down his brow. She was about to ask if something was wrong when he spoke. "Can I touch your breasts?" Even at fifteen, with no experience besides a hurried kiss behind the bleachers, she was stunned that he could pose such a question without thinking to kiss her first, to touch her hair. She knew she was weak enough that she would have been less resistant had the request followed a moment of physical tenderness. But he had framed it so she would have had to be worse than weak to comply. So she said "No," feeling hurt, yet also pleased by the calm in her voice, "I don't think that would be a good idea." Though her knees were wobbly, she managed to resume the conversation right where they left off.

It was one of those rare moments that Libby felt, in spite of her pain, she had handled well. But when she came to school the next day, Libby realized there had been no correct response. For Dusty spent the entire day making fun of her. Obviously his strategy was to prevent her from revealing his weakness by discrediting her first. She hadn't planned to tell anyone, but now she *knew* she couldn't; the truth was trapped inside her; no one would believe her and even if they did, she would be humiliated. When Dusty became particularly nasty, Susan had pulled Libby aside, against the lockers, and apologized: "I don't know what's gotten into him today; sometimes he just needs to pick on someone. It's nothing personal. I know he likes you." For the first time, Libby had known the true nature of a secret, the pain of needing to tell, but not being able to.

What Libby could not know either that day as they stood by the straight rows of military-gray lockers or now—as she and Maudie left the boys behind to walk ahead to the water tower—was that her favorite field was not permanently ruined for her. Because in a year, when she became sixteen, a boy she loved would take Libby, in a special flowered sundress she had borrowed from Maudie, to that very field. The purple clover would be the thickest she would ever see it, so frothy that it looked like the flowers were bubbling over. Together they would lie down, the fragrance of clover and rich Illinois earth so overwhelming that they would almost become dizzy from the smell, the steady hum of insects, the buzz of bees. As dusk descended, they would make first love, their bodies adjusting to one another allowing them to unravel again and again, flattening the matted weeds, reshaping the earth. When finally they would rise, they would see the borrowed dress was ruined, stained with grass and blood.

"Don't worry," the boy would say, for he would be a farm boy, different from the village kids. "It will come out. I'll give you a solution we use." Then, wrapping his shirt around her waist, bending to knot it in the front, he would add, "For now, take this." Together they would walk up the slope, around to the front of the barn, across the gravel road to his car, an old Chevy with fins. He would open the door for her and kiss each of her fingers before she climbed inside, a sweet gesture because it was both contrived and natural. After he turned on the radio, they would sit and listen, the boy holding her tight to his side. When "Love Me Do" came on, the boy would take out an invisible harmonica and she would ask, before she had a chance to think, "What happened to your guitar?" Without acting like it was an unusual question, the boy would respond, "I prefer a harmonica to a guitar. It takes more care. Did you know you have to keep it by your bed in a glass of water overnight to keep the reeds moist?" She would love the way he said guitar, "gee-tar," so different from the village boys. And she would find the information about harmonica reeds the greatest wisdom ever imparted. She would be the happiest she had ever been as she watched his dancing fingers slide the invisible instrument against his lips.

But since Libby could know none of this on her way to the water tower, she simply said, "God, I can't stand Dusty Walker."

"Oh, I think he's kinda cute," said Maudie. "You just don't like him 'cause of that one time, you know, that day by the lockers last spring."

"Maybe," said Libby, considering, as she had many times, telling Maudie, then deciding against it. Though she was Libby's best friend, she wasn't great with secrets. They were almost to the closest leg of the tower. "Do you want to smoke a cigarette before we change?"

"Sure," said Maudie, pulling a crushed pack from her hip pocket, and handing Libby a flattened cigarette.

They leaned against the enormous steel leg of the tower, quietly smoking. Holding the cigarette between her ring and middle fingers, Libby gently waved her hand. The burning tip became a supernatural jeweled ring that shed trails—brilliant amber streamers—when it moved. She was transfixed for only a moment before shifting to her haunches to take a long drag. As the smoke filled her lungs, she was imbued with a strange mixture of longing and dread. She knew it was foolish to swim inside the tower. She knew but couldn't turn back. Libby looked up and saw the dim shape of the boys coming toward them. They had finished cavorting and were ready for the tower. Libby crushed the butt out in the dirt.

"Let's step into the woods to change," she said.

"Uh-huh," said Maudie, as she flicked the stub of her cigarette in an arc across the night sky. Casey McIntyre clapped hollowly at the brief light show. The ember sizzled and blinked in the grass before dying.

In the woods, the girls lifted their blouses over their heads.

"Hey Maudie, hurry it up!" called Casey.

"I think he likes you," whispered Libby.

"Me too," said Maudie and they both giggled.

When they stripped, Libby was surprised that Maudie wasn't wearing her suit under her clothing. Instead she wore just a bra and panties. In Hubbard's Drug Store, Casey had tried to convince them that underwear was as good as a swimsuit. Obviously he had succeeded with Maudie. To Libby, it felt odd to be standing in a suit at night on a matted forest bed of old leaves and broken twigs. She wondered if Maudie felt uncomfortable now that it was actually time to leave the woods. But as with so many of the things she couldn't know that night, she couldn't know that in just a few years she and Maudie would no longer be friends. And Maudie, who had always squatted inches above toilet seats to avoid germs, would have slept with close to fifty boys. Libby would be one of the only ones in their crowd who hadn't "gone bad," as the parents said, drinking, drugs, or worse. But that night, they were both still innocent.

As Libby and Maudie emerged from the woods, Dusty said, out of the corner of his mouth, "Figures she's wearing a suit, and a one-piece at that." Libby pretended not to hear him. At least she didn't have to fold her arms across her breasts the way Maudie did. Besides, the boys looked less threatening in their underpants than she would have guessed. Gleaming in the moonlight, their legs looked long and chalky, like the stick legs of awkward young colts. Libby glanced away.

"Well?" asked Casey. He shot his cigarette in the air—a sparkling arc—as Maudie had done just moments before, and gestured to Maudie, a footman's exaggerated bow, for her to begin her ascent. Such gallantry seemed silly coming from a boy wearing nothing but short white briefs. It didn't matter; Maudie was clearly charmed. She started up the ladder, Casey right beneath her. Once they were six feet off the ground, Casey looked back over his shoulder, the right side of his face illuminated by the moon, his eye crystal, yet as blue-white as his cheek. "So?" he said. "What are you guys waiting for?"

Like goldfish drawn to a single crumb, the group converged at the ladder's base, Dusty and Libby at precisely the same moment, his arm brushing hers as he grasped the side railing. She shivered.

"Oh, excuse me, you go ahead," she said, glancing away.

"No, I wouldn't dream of it," he said sarcastically. She felt his warm breath on her hair, her heart pounding. She stepped in front of him onto the first rung. Libby was startled to see how straight the ladder was, perfectly vertical. She had to turn slightly sideways to climb in order to allow room for her knees not to scrap the rungs. Dusty followed her. She felt uneasy with him immediately beneath her, almost touching, his arms encircling her calves. But what could she do? Besides, it was better than having no one to cushion the fall. She looked up at the ladder rising above her in a straight line and felt

WHERE YOU CAN'T TOUCH BOTTOM   119

dizzy. She paused. She wanted to back down. But she knew the line of boys beneath her wouldn't descend to make way for her.

"Don't stop," commanded Dusty, and then, in a gentler voice, "and don't look up or down."

He was right. If she stared straight ahead, the rush in her belly subsided. She climbed until she felt Maudie reaching down to help pull her up the rest of the way.

The group crowded onto the scaffolding hugging the tank. While Casey gave instructions, the rest stood at attention, a solemn ceremony. Afterwards, Casey removed the door to the tank, causing a great scraping noise that sent shivers down Libby's spine. Randy tied a rope end around the railing and tossed the tail into the dark hole. A plopping noise soon followed.

"It's really full tonight," he said.

"Uh-huh," agreed Casey. "They must have just filled it."

"Who first?" asked Maudie.

"I'll go," said Randy. He shifted his long exposed legs onto the ledge, squatted, then dove, making a wonderfully hollow splashing noise.

"I'll be the first lookout," said Sam.

"Maudie, you and Libby go next," said Casey.

Maudie climbed up, then pushed away, holding her knees, cannonball-style. Libby took her spot on the ledge and looked down. Except for a circle of rippling moonlight on the dark water, the interior was pitch black.

"You guys outta the way?" she shouted into the hole.

"Yeah, come on," Maudie called back, her words echoing.

"Is it better to dive or jump?" asked Libby, knowing she couldn't stall forever.

"It doesn't matter," said Randy, another echo from the darkness. "It's really deep. You couldn't touch bottom if you wanted to."

Without thinking, Libby pushed forward with her feet. Her stomach soared. Diving was like plunging into a void. Hitting water was a surprise, yet her outstretched arms opened quickly, automatically, dividing the liquid, drawing her deeper. She kicked to propel herself to the surface. Her right arm swept against a floating object—a flake of rust, she imagined, drifting aimlessly like an industrial lily pad. Never had she felt so suspended. Except for the single shaft of light illuminating the dangling rope, she was in utter blackness. Her feet could not touch bottom and there were no railings or edges to cling to, only huge curving walls. Holding her hand an inch from her face, she could not see it. A big splash was followed by another burst, then another, then nothing but the rippling sounds of the other swimmers, their reverberating voices.

"This is so weird," said Maudie. "I can't see a thing; the air blends right into the water—you can't tell where one ends."

"Hey," said Randy, "who wants to play blindman's bluff?"

"I'm It," shouted Dusty. "No one's allowed to go into the light."

"Roll call first," said Casey. Everyone called their names.

"Okay," said Randy. *"Go!"*

"Blindman's!" cried Dusty.

What sounded like a dozen "bluffs" answered, resounding off the curved walls. Everyone dispersed, sending a series of waves, purling out, slapping the walls. Libby swam as hard as she could against the tide, but she seemed not to move at all. When she finally felt safe enough to pause, she was weak. If only she had some support for a moment, anything to clutch.

"I got you; I got someone," said Dusty.

"My ankle," said Maudie.

"You're It."

"Blindman's!"

"Bluff!" shouted the others. Again, it was difficult to tell where the voices originated. Libby saw her fingers flash momentarily in the light, like touching fire, then swam in the opposite direction, toward the blackness, an odd sensation, like swimming in india ink, solid pigment, from nothing, to nothing. The water surged in all different directions like a pot being stirred. Libby was tossed one way, then another.

"I can't get anyone," sighed Maudie. "I'm confused."

"Over here, I'm to your left," said Casey.

"Libby, where are you?" asked Maudie.

Libby opened her mouth to answer, but no words came out. She found she was weaker, her arms and legs drained. She attempted to move in the direction of Maudie's voice, but her limbs were powerless, empty. She was afraid to speak, *couldn't* speak, as if it would exhaust her breath, take the last of it. She wiggled her feet, but her legs wouldn't follow. No matter how hard she tried to reach Maudie, she remained almost stationary, unable to close any space.

WHERE YOU CAN'T TOUCH BOTTOM 121

She realized her error; with what little strength she had, she should have tried to reach the rope instead of Maudie. Now she didn't have the energy for either. Regardless of how hard she tried to kick, her legs sank. The water seemed as thick as mud, like it was sucking her under.

"Libby?" Maudie called again, panic rising in her voice.

"We better do a roll call," said Casey. Libby could hear the water lapping softly as everyone treaded in place, responding to their names, everyone except Libby. She couldn't afford the breath. There was no way to signal; words would not come.

"Oh God, where's Libby?" asked Maudie, near hysteria. *"Lib-bee, Lib-bee, answer, right this minute, Lib-beeee."*

"What's the matter down there?" called Sam. Libby could see the silhouette of his head and shoulders against the night sky.

"We can't find Libb," said Randy, his voice weak.

Their voices faded. Libby was completely vertical now, her body trailing from her head like weighted ribbon, her feet barely swaying, her head thrown back, face turned upward, a small island above the surface. She knew if she called out she would forfeit the last of her strength and drown; if, instead, she saved her breath she couldn't be found and rescued. There was nothing to do.

"Libbbeee, Libbbeee," Maudie was crying.

The others joined in, a chorus singing her name: strung together over and over, it sounded like a strange word.

Libby's feet dangled like dumbbells. She hadn't known she could be so removed from her body while so controlled by it. Water trickled into her mouth, then rushed down her throat. Her head sank and was swallowed. She gurgled and followed the pull of her feet.

Something—a hand—touched her arm, then grabbed it.

"I've got her!" called Casey. "Quick! Over here!"

In a flurry of splashes, it seemed like a million hands were on her—the hands of her past, her present, and her future. She was an infant sleeping in a dresser drawer at the end of her parents' bed; a girl sipping a soda in Hubbard's Drug Store; a girl-woman making love with the farm boy; a woman leaving home for college, making decisions, going places; a woman marrying, bearing children, divorcing, finding fresh love, mature love, all without ever touching bottom. She knew she could hold on while letting go. Though it would never happen again, it was all right—for all the moments of her life came together in that one moment, encapsuled in a single swirling second, when mystery and wonder were no longer outgrowths of fear and weakness, but entities she could own, even while surrendering herself to the churning water and the multitude of hands.

Appetites

Tommy's mother, Agnes, watches him popping up in the pool at the motel where they are staying with her fiancé, Frank, and his two daughters. Tommy's movements are so powerful that it is as if he were being shot upward rather than being propelled by his own strength. Each time, his arms pressed tighter to his sides, he rises higher, jerking his head to the right to keep the wet hair from his eyes. His bangs, much longer than the rest of his hair, coil on top of his head, reminding Agnes of swirls of frozen custard as they wind from the dispenser into cones. The brightness of the water, intensified by lights below the surface, and of the clear summer sky looks almost unreal. This makes Tommy's thin chest, naked against all this artificial blueness, seem slightly obscene. It is as if a real nine-year-old boy has forced his way into the unnatural colors of a Disney cartoon. Agnes wants to look away, but there is nothing else to watch. He is the only one in the pool. Finally, teeth clenched in a frown of exertion, chin pressed to his neck, Tommy makes his final and highest emergence. The waterline meets his thighs; then he falls back down and swims, a ripple of flesh beneath the surface, toward the end of the pool.

"Agnes . . . Aggie," says a small voice at her elbow, making her jump. She feels the same guilt that she did when she was a girl and her mother walked in on her cheating at solitaire: a guilt no one could ever prove.

"When we gonna go to dinner?" asks the girl at her elbow.

"I promised Tommy he could swim until six-fifteen."

They both watch the water ripple in silence.

"He sure can jump high," says the girl.

This makes Agnes feel less disloyal in her critical observation of Tommy; she knows that Tommy would never be so generous in his remarks about either this girl or her younger sister.

"What's your daddy doing?"

"He's back in our room with Beth. He let us put a quarter in the bed and sit on it while it jiggled."

The motel sits in a bowl-shaped valley. The bunchy foliage of the trees on the surrounding slopes reminds Agnes of freshly washed broccoli. If she squints just the right way it seems as if she could reach out and touch it: crumble it in her fingers. There is nothing else in the valley besides the motel and a battered old amusement park they pass on their way to the caves. In a way, the trip is a vacation. Each day, they select a different guided tour, going deeper into the caves, examining the mysteries of older and better stalactites with two hundred other people. In another way, the trip is a test to see how the children get along—a test to see how things will work out if she and Frank actually do get married.

"Tommy! Tommy!" she calls, wondering if her words look like rippled cartoon words as they travel beneath the surface to her son. Tommy breaks the smooth sheet of water, suddenly, just as she is about to call again, then circles the pool twice in splashy breaststrokes before climbing out.

On the other side of the valley they go to a restaurant with a Japanese-Chinese motif called the House of Jade. There are plastic renditions of paper lanterns in the center of each table, Foo Dog salt and pepper shakers, and twisted ceramic dragons, the size of two year olds, on either side of the cashier's desk and coffee station. As soon as they have ordered their drinks, Tommy neatly refolds his red napkin and excuses himself. This is something he does every place they go, even the caves—he needs to see the rest rooms first.

"We'll have to break him of that," says Frank, the girls' father, watching Tommy's hips weave through the tables covered in black cloths. Agnes thinks about asking why but doesn't. She is sorry that she pointed the ritual out to Frank the night before, sure that he wouldn't have noticed otherwise. It was a momentary, inverted sense of pride. Through a series of associations, the ritual had reminded her of Tommy's real father. He used to say his teeth ached when he needed to urinate and there was no place to go. Usually quick to censor vulgar clichés, Agnes had ignored that one, thinking of the way her own teeth and gums seemed to swell and contract in the act of love. She thought that somehow all parts of the body called to, and responded to, other parts of the body when in need. It wasn't until years later that someone told her "aching teeth" was only an expression that men use.

"They call the men's room 'Guys' and the girls' room 'Geishas,' " says Tommy as he pulls out his chair and resumes his place in the group. "It's really no better than a gas-station rest room. There's nothing Japanese about it at all. At the airport, they have bull's-eye targets over the urinals."

"Tommy," begins Frank, looking stern and fatherly, "you're going to have to maintain some control over how often you go to the rest room."

"Oakley's grandfather has *no* control and has a hole cut in his side with a sack over it," answers Tommy, purposely misunderstanding. His eyes are glazed like those of a drunken man. He leans slightly forward, his fingertips appearing just over the edge of the table. Agnes sees his father stagger in her mind.

"Yuck!" screams the older of the two girls. "Is it see-through?"

"*Enough*," says Frank, looking at Tommy, "and you know exactly what I mean." His thinning hair is strawberry blond but looks orange against his flush of anger.

"Can I have a hamburger?" asks the younger girl.

"I think it would be more appropriate to *try* something Oriental as long as we're here," says Frank, opening his large menu in a way that signals a new beginning.

Agnes looks at the three children. The girls look like the photographs she has seen of their mother. Tommy looks like his father. She has heard of couples with opposing views not voting because they would only cancel each other out. She wonders, with children so unlike them and they so unlike each other, if they as a family would all eventually cancel one another out.

"It *is* Oriental. Listen," says the girl and reads from the menu: "Hong Kong Hamburger."

Nothing on the menu, it turns out, is really Oriental. It is all just made to sound that way. The children have the hamburgers.

Frank has the Lotus Lamb Chops and Agnes orders the Oriental Omelet. She wishes the drinks had little paper parasols in them. As a child, she would twirl the thin ribbed poles between her fingertips until the miniature designs of the shades melted into spinning bands.

This is the third day of their vacation. On the first two days, immediately after the tours, they had returned to the motel to swim. Today, as a surprise, Frank took them to the wax museum. Agnes felt Tommy was disappointed that it was an educational museum rather than a Ripley's Believe It or Not, like the one with the three-headed cow in Gatlinburg—even though he was only two when she had taken him there and probably couldn't remember it.

Frank bought the magic key for the explanation boxes that were beside each of the glass-enclosed scenes, but the voices were scratchy and inaudible, so he had to explain each one anyway. At first there seemed to be some plan behind the grouping of exhibits: English royalty with a backdrop of castle walls, Civil War heroes bunched together outside a tent. But as they passed through the halls, the scenes became disjointed. The glass rooms became larger and in-cluded more figures. People didn't seem to belong together. Sleeping Beauty appeared with Mickey Mantle. Some characters seemed to be talking, but were facing a wall. Others were laughing but sitting alone. It was as if the designer had become rushed or bored.

"I bet if they made what all these people are saying outta wax it would look like melted globs hanging in the air," said Tommy.

"You can't *see* words," said Frank, producing an artificial chuckle.

"I can," said Tommy.

Frank decided to let this one go and stooped to tie the younger girl's shoe. Over Frank's curved back, Tommy quickly knotted the air, making an imaginary noose, stuck his head inside, and drew the cord. He let his head roll, like a basketball on the rim, around his shoulders, until Frank stood up.

On the ride from the restaurant back to the motel, Agnes can't help but recall when riding was a way of life and staying still was a vacation. It was a time when they subsisted on the wares of dusty roadside stands and Dairy Queens. She remembers Tommy's father behind the wheel, Tommy asleep in her lap. He had been sucking a cherry Popsicle. His lips were crimson. With his pale skin, perfect features, and feverish cheeks, he reminded her of a photograph from the forties that had been retouched. She could imagine the photographers dabbing the color on his lips with a paintbrush as pointed as a mermaid's nipple.

Agnes remembers stroking his hair when suddenly he shot up, his open eyes the brilliant green of GO lights swinging against a storm. His body produced a violent shake. He heaved forward. Automatically, Agnes cupped her hands beneath his lips. Transparent fluid, the hue of the melted Popsicle, gushed into the bowl of her hands. She held the vomit for almost a mile, not knowing what to do with it, staring at the pink bubbles, before Tommy's father said, "Throw it out the window," and she did. They were driving so fast that she didn't even hear the splat.

When they drive past the amusement park on their way to the motel, Tommy presses his face against the glass as if he were seeing the rides for the first time.

"Why don't we go there?" he asks.

"No," says Agnes, "it looks too rickety."

"Just for a little while?"

"No," adds Frank.

"Why don't we just take a couple of rides and if we don't like them we don't have to take any more," says Tommy. "You know, like *test rides.*"

"Your mother said no," Frank says, reddening a little. He doesn't catch Tommy's allusion, but senses the challenge in his tone. Tommy moves out of Frank's field of vision in the rearview mirror, looks at his mother, and rolls his eyes. He shapes his hand like a gun, puts his finger to his temple, and pulls the trigger. His head slumps to his shoulder and he runs his fingers down his face, simulating streaming blood.

"It's not far," says Agnes. "Maybe Tommy and I will just walk back up and take a few rides."

Frank sighs. Tommy comes to life again, but only to shoot himself once more.

"We won't be gone long," says Agnes.

"Can we go too?" ask the girls in unison.

"No," Frank says as he turns the wheel sharply into the motel parking lot. The car dips to the left, then to the right over the crunchy piles of gravel. Agnes imagines that the rear fenders look like a pair of wide hips from behind.

"You can just let us out here," says Tommy, confident, his eyes crossed and his finger pointed at his temple, but still sitting where Frank can't see him.

Frank ignores him and pulls up to the slot in front of their adjoining rooms. The pointy stucco walls make Agnes think of plaster that hadn't quite dried before hundreds of children attacked it and patted it with the open palms of their hands. She can't decide whether to slam the car door, matching Frank's anger, or to act gracious. She chooses the latter and walks in quick, delicate steps around the car to meet Frank as he gets out. Her flesh-colored shoes make her feet appear naked. She kisses the soft skin beneath his eyes and realizes that the test is just a pretense conceived by them both. It is really her choice. He may not be as exciting as others, but she will finally have a sense of control. Over Frank's shoulder she sees Tommy emptying the cylinder of the imaginary revolver.

When they are alone on the dirt road to the amusement park, Agnes thinks about lecturing Tommy, but can't. He is himself again: a child. Even his voice changes.

"Tell me again," he asks, kicking the ruts in the road, "how did my father die?"

It is not the first time he has tried to catch her this way.

"I've told you before. He isn't dead. He just up and left, took off, disappeared." She wants to accent this statement with her hand opening quickly in the air, like a single kernel of popcorn bursting from its seed, and the word *poof*. But out of respect for Tommy, she refrains.

"Where did Frank's wife go?" he asks.

"She didn't leave," says Agnes. "She's dead."

The amusement park is very old and small. The roller coaster is wooden and unpainted, with a sign that says OUT OF ORDER. Agnes doesn't think it would take more than one match. While Tommy goes to the portable red outhouse, Agnes buys the tickets from an old woman with a dried-apple face in a booth painted with faded stars. The woman doesn't say anything. She simply slides the six tickets across the narrow counter. Their texture reminds Agnes of the soft cardboard that egg cartons are made of.

APPETITES 129

"Well, how was it?" she asks Tommy as he emerges.

He shrugs and shakes his head. "Different than you would expect. It's really clean and has paper birds hanging from the ceiling. Do you know which ride you want to try first?"

"It's up to you."

"One of these, I guess," says Tommy, indicating the hanging helicopters or the twirling saucers. An attendant is standing between the two rides, so Agnes asks him if he runs them both.

"Yeah," he says, smiling widely.

She can tell from his empty eyes that he isn't all there. She also knows, from experience, that it is a happy emptiness, not the kind that is waiting to be filled with another's agony. He has probably been operating the rides for years.

"The saucer?" she asks Tommy.

"Okay," he says.

"You can go for a long time," says the attendant as he secures the metal bar across their laps, "as long as no one else don't come."

The ride goes slowly at first, then picks up speed. Tommy shrieks; his curved hands slide down the bar as he is pushed against her. She is on the outside and the centrifugal force works to push her harder against the wall. Tommy is pressed into her side, laughing: a child's laughter. Agnes laughs too as she feels her hair whip against her face. She notices that the attendant is right. There is no one else there. Not only are they the only customers but he is the only attendant. The ride goes on for so long that Agnes waves at him to stop it. He is leaning, cross-armed, against a pole. He sees her, smiles, and waves back. This makes Tommy, who understands, laugh harder. Agnes tries to rise, waving both arms, pointing toward the controls, but is pushed back. Her neck seems about to snap like a rubber band, and her laughter, like Tommy's, is lost to the motion. In a blur, she sees the attendant move toward the throttle. Tommy is molded to her side. The ride seems to pick up speed, then slows.

Her jaw aches from laughter and her teeth feel dry. She thinks of Frank, his thinning hair neatly arranged across his scalp, waiting in the motel room. Then an image of Tommy's father comes to her. She sees him sitting behind the wheel, one elbow resting on the open window. She sees his dark hair rising from his off-center part like a wedge of cake placed on its side, and feels hungry.

Fabric

"So, what did you think?" asks Teresa, hoping her voice doesn't sound too cheerful, too anxious. The sun was setting when they entered the theater—streaks of tangerine, red and peacock blue bleeding together, like a gigantic tie-dye T-shirt stretched between buildings. Now the street is dark. They stride past shadowy alleys. Headlights flash and glitter against the purple night, brooches for the deep sky's suit. The world was one place when they entered, another when they emerged. Teresa used to like this sensation. Now it bothers her that she only looks away briefly and everything changes.

"The dog was pretty cool," says Paul. "Overall an interesting point of view."

What dog? Teresa wants to ask, but knows Paul will sigh wearily. He considers his critical talents superior to hers. He never even leaves the theater until all the credits have rolled. *"Film people care about every last production assistant. They need to know."* Usually Teresa balks at this pretension. Tonight she sat quietly, as if intrigued by the names— like ashes from a fire, drifting upward—while secretly observing the ushers in their ill-fitting tuxedos. Gawky pimpled youths, they stood in the doors waiting while the overhead lights rose in intensity, then tackled the rows with brooms and Hefty bags. Even in their odd attire, they resembled medics—called away from balls and proms— to gather remains after a disaster. The black ribbon riding their lapels glinted as they worked.

Teresa chooses the same strategy now. Instead of inquiring about the dog, she locks her hands behind her back, leans forward, and

FABRIC 131

watches the sidewalk rush beneath their feet. Mica sparkles. Cement awash with diamonds. The image hits her full in the face: her mother's evening-party top, a sleeveless sequin shell, a billion shimmering discs, overlapping one another, central holes threaded creating a drape of insect record albums that conceal the cloth to which they're strung. Teresa nearly stumbles. Her heart aches.

Lately Teresa's train of thought is often interrupted by visions of fabric from her past. The images feel too fresh, too intense, to be called recollections. Not memories of memories, but impressions recovered after long submersion beneath layers of experience. Fabric flashbacks. Triggered by everyday sights, the images appear without warning. She sees a swatch of material or an item of clothing—a wool coat hanging from a store rack, a dress clinging to a subway passenger, a blouse in a magazine advertisement, a curtain panel uplifted by a gentle breeze—and is immediately thrown back in time, the vision before her eyes. The fabric overwhelms her with its presence: the colors, smell, feel between her fingers, the weave of the cloth magnified. She becomes who she was then, the girl in the fourth-grade play, an embroidered rose growing up her silk belly. She smells the lemon wax of the church as she walked down the aisle wearing her white confirmation dress. The day comes flooding back. Teresa sitting in the hard pew, studying the floral designs of the bobbin-lace overlay, the intertwisting mesh of delicate threads. She recalls the pleasant feeling of her breasts swelling beneath the orange sleeveless turtleneck she wore when her hoody boyfriend, Kevin, pressed her against the garage wall for her first serious kiss. His calloused hands on her bare shoulders. The flaking paint of the garage, the pungent odor of the leaf mulch at their feet. She sees Paul and herself in a more carefree time, strolling down the street— wearing the tie-dyes they had made together in her backyard from cheap men's undershirts—barefoot in blue jeans, the soles of her feet against the hot concrete, the feel of the air, as if anything might happen, could happen, indeed, *would* happen. Her head hurts to recall such moments.

"Do you want to try Juan's?" she asks. Juan's used to be their favorite Mexican restaurant: plain with a linoleum floor, long card tables, and flickering lights, but authentic. After graduation but before Lucy was born, they had liked to drink Juan's margaritas and order the big fish he served in molded tin-foil trays. They had dipped the white meat in the butter and garlic collected in the silver folds. The ritual had reminded them of their honeymoon in Mérida. Teresa quickly calculates. At least three years have passed since they last ate at Juan's. Eight since their honeymoon.

"Why not?" Paul shrugs, disinterested. His attitude is not fair. They agreed to have this weekend alone to rekindle the relationship, see what was left to salvage. But they are not alone. The woman he met in L.A. joins them, her specter between them as they walk the three blocks to Juan's. Teresa can see that Paul isn't trying, just traveling the motions so he can say he did. But she will make him, snap him out of this ridiculous infatuation. An actress! How could he take up with an actress ten years his junior when he has a four-year-old daughter at home? But those are Teresa's mother's words. Teresa understands; he wants to stop time. He thinks he can reclaim his youth. Why not? It wasn't so very long ago, and at the time, they had thought their state was permanent—that being twenty-five was a characteristic they possessed like brown eyes, fair skin, a hearty laugh. Some people were tall, some were twenty-five. If people could lose weight, regain their youthful figures, why not lose years? And just like dieters were foolish to hang out with big eaters, wouldn't he be stupid to lug around someone with an affliction similar to his own?

Teresa discovered the affair three weeks ago. Unloading the groceries, she had found a black and white photograph of the woman tucked beneath the carpeting in the car trunk. Paul was so foolish. It was such an obvious publicity shot, he could have propped the picture on their dresser and Teresa wouldn't have questioned it, just thought it was the one that came with the frame. But the hidden photo, in connection to all his recent trips to L.A., left no other possibility. Though now, Teresa regrets mentioning the photograph. Perhaps if she hadn't confronted him, his romance would have run its course. But she had chosen to make a dramatic scene, ripping the photo into fluttering shreds. Regardless, the woman's face burns indelibly in Teresa's memory. Beneath chopped blond hair, bright eyes stare from a clean face, square as a pocket of a starched white shirt. Teresa imagines the woman in her mother's sequin top—the burst of dazzling sequins. The men in the movie they saw earlier would have dropped their guns at such beauty. But what about the dog?

FABRIC

133

· · ·

Stepping over the threshold into Juan's brings instant disappoint-ment. Though the restaurant is still called Juan's, Juan has clearly departed. The once funky interior has been redecorated to resem-ble a popular franchise. Bright wooden parrots and piñatas swing from the ceiling. The tablecloths are brilliant red, green, yellow, and pink. Waitresses wearing full fiesta skirts and peasant blouses whirl past. Embroidered flowers decorate the blouses' smocking. Teresa envisions a Mexican blouse she purchased on her honeymoon, the scoop of the neck, her tanned collarbone. The smell of sea and suntan lotion. Walking along the cool beach at night, barefoot, again in faded jeans, the sand still warm from the heat of the day. She had felt exotic in that blouse. Because of her name, people frequently ask if she is Latina. She always wishes she could answer yes, but the truth is her mother is Irish Catholic, her father was Jewish. They had named her sister Pam, her brother Bob. Teresa has no idea why her mother chose "Teresa" for her. When she asked, her mother simply said it was pretty.

"We don't have to stay," says Paul.

"We're here, it's almost eight, we might as well try it," says Teresa. She immediately regrets her words. Everything she says is loaded. Right before Teresa discovered the other woman, Paul had declared they needed to postpone their dinner hour to a more civilized time. He was so adamant that Teresa began making two separate dinners, one for Lucy at five-thirty and one for her and Paul at eight. After all, he was the one working to get a fledgling business off the ground. The project in L.A. was his first big job. Most of the commercials he directed were shot right here in Chicago. If he needed warm weather, he shot in Florida where costs are cheaper. But this client insisted on L.A. *and* on Paul. Was it a scheme concocted to bring Paul and the actress together? Teresa laughs aloud at the idea.

"What?" asks Paul.

"Nothing," says Teresa. The hostess, a heavy woman, bleached blond with blue-rimmed glasses, has arrived.

The food tastes mundane, not bad enough to laugh at, or leave, just plain bland. Paul picks at his burrito, his mind obviously with the actress, thinking what a great restaurant they would choose, what a wonderful time they would share. Teresa thinks about stabbing him with a fork, but knows that isn't what she really wants. She wants him to recognize the possibilities in her, see what he used to see. Laugh the way he used to laugh. She can't believe she is in such a situation. Ten years ago when she met Paul, they were both graduate film students. She had planned on an exciting life, different from her mother's.

Her mother, Teresa knew, was beautiful when she married Teresa's father. She had seen photographs. In her favorite, her mother wore a striped sundress with a cinched belt and full skirt. Her father clasped her mother's tiny waist, the perfect handle for his huge fingers. Teresa had studied the Veronica Lake dip of her mother's flaxen hair. Her father, too, was handsome. Rich brown curls. A toothy salesman's grin. Teresa knew he was once considered lively and ambitious, well worth her mother defying her parents to marry him.

A salesman at Marshall Field's, promoted to buyer, he opened his own store when Teresa was still a baby. But by the time her younger sister, Pam, was born he was already on his way to ruin. No one ever told Teresa what had happened, but she picked up bits and pieces. Shadowy conversations. Whispers of her friends' parents. The biggest clue came when she walked in on an argument her mother and grandmother were having in the kitchen.

Her mother stood at the sink wiping dishes, her back perfectly straight, her eyes staring over the heads of the plastic Virgin Mary and saints lining the windowsill, out into the backyard. She appeared to be trying to ignore her mother, a snarling woman hunched over like a turtle from osteoporosis. Teresa's mother had finally snapped when her grandmother said "Jewish lightning." But she had stopped cold when she saw Teresa in the doorway, leaving the expression unexplained, open to Teresa's own interpretation. Teresa imagined a war between the Jewish God and the Catholic God, each heaving enormous bolts of lightning at the other until one struck her father's store, burning it to the ground. Later she learned her father's store had been set on fire by his partner. Arson for the insurance money. Her father was eventually cleared, but the store and money were lost.

The entire family had moved in with Teresa's grandmother. The arrangement was supposed to be temporary, but Teresa's father was so demoralized that he never found another full-time job. Her grandmother's sofa took on the shape of her father napping, the indentation of his body. In her mind's eye, Teresa can clearly see the scooped hollow in the pea-green sofa, speckled with the little white cotton nubs of his molting undershirt. By the time he died an early death at forty-five, he had so ceased to exist in Teresa's mind that Teresa was actually stunned by the extent of her mother's grief. How could a nonentity's demise create such a void, invoke such pain and loss?

Her parents' history, Teresa knew, was partly what attracted her to Paul in the first place. One of the more talented students in their program—and by far the most exuberant and self-confident—he was clearly going places. And she would go with him. They were going to make esoteric little films, only black and whites. To finance their art, he would write Hollywood scripts.

As it turned out, Teresa works twenty hours a week as a researcher in a film library while Paul shoots commercials. Until recently, Paul liked to boast that at least they're both still in the industry, not sell-outs. What does he think commercials are? And worse, they are sell-outs without money. If Paul leaves her she will be lucky if she doesn't have to move back home with her mother.

"Don't you think it's time we talk?" she asks, leaning across the bright pink tablecloth. Her head throbs from the memory of a radiant pink linen suit she owned in high school. She wore matching pink lipstick smelling of cheap perfume.

With fork prongs, Paul rakes at his burrito stuffing. He shrugs, then looks her in the eyes.

"What about? It's clear we're not clicking."

"That's not fair," she says, thinking *Nothing is fair in love and war.* "You're not putting your heart in it."

"I can't control my heart," says Paul, looking back at the burrito. Ground beef tumbles out. Teresa thinks of the puffy arm of an old down jacket he used to own, the way the frayed cuff looked when the insulation began to leak. Teresa marvels at how easily the flashbacks come now, how strange that the images are of fabric, given she has never sewed or had any interest in fashion. Paul used to laugh at her lack of fashion sense, her mismatched outfits. Now his affectionate teasing has turned to plain criticism. *"You're not going to the dinner party in that, are you?"* Teresa's father always noticed when his wife dressed up. He used to whistle when Teresa's mother put on the sequin shell for a rare night out, as if his former self had been momentarily awakened. Until recently Teresa could not have been convinced that any aspect of her mother's life was enviable.

"We're just not having any fun," says Paul.

Fun? The word seems curious to Teresa. A concept she hasn't considered in ages. As if to illustrate, a group of waiters and waitresses surround the neighboring table where a party of four is eating dinner. A short waiter places an oversized sombrero on the head of one of the diners, a man with a pencil mustache and faintly pockmarked checks. While the waiter and the hefty hostess shake maracas, the rest of the staff breaks into "Happy Birthday." The short waiter quickly snaps a Polaroid of the man in the sombrero. Teresa smiles at the gaiety. The lilt of their rising voices. The drooping sombrero.

Once, early in their marriage, Teresa had surprised Paul at a restaurant with the delivery of a cupcake with a candle. Teresa and two young waitresses both in ruffled white blouses sang "Happy Birthday." Paul was embarrassed—a deep blush spread up his neck, like linen absorbing wine—but happy. Flushed and happy. Was the restaurant on Halsted? Teresa couldn't remember. Only the hue of Paul's neck, the white waitress blouses against their black pants. The fine weave of the tablecloth. Cream linen.

She should have continued the birthday tradition. A trail of restaurants, a chain of birthday songs, and laughter. Teresa couldn't remember how they celebrated Paul's birthday this year. She wasn't even sure of his age. Thirty-three or thirty-four? They were so young when they met. *They are still young.* Maybe, Teresa decides, she is to blame for the actress.

"Perhaps we *should* talk," says Paul. "We have to consider Lucy. Make sure this doesn't affect her."

Using Lucy as an excuse for a clean getaway seems obscene.

"How can this not affect her?" asks Teresa.

All of a sudden her situation appears clear; she and Lucy will be forced to move home with her mother. Into the very house her mother had retreated to after her husband failed, the white stucco two-story west of Ashland that *still* smells of her grandmother. Teresa wonders if she will have to share her room with Pam, who returned home after college. Or will Teresa and Lucy share? Either possibility depresses Teresa. Pam has gained thirty pounds in the three years since her return. Ten a year. It was too sad, the thought of them, three women and a girl—three generations—living in that house.

Her brother, Bob, is in Missouri now with his own family: a wife and two children.

In the home of her youth, Teresa will be forced to relive the past daily. Her mother and grandmother's hissed arguments in the kitchen. She will watch Lucy play in the spot of long grass under the apple tree where she and Paul had tie-dyed T-shirts; she will weed in the first place they made love, under protection of the side porch latticework. Hear the rattle of the El less than two blocks away. Serve meals in the very dining room where they held her grandmother's wake. Park her car in the garage where she and her hoody boyfriend, Kevin, kissed.

Teresa repeats her question. "How can this not affect her?" asks Teresa.

Paul sighs. Teresa detests his new way of sighing. His lips part, the broad lower lip falling, like a seam coming apart in his face—the first slow tear.

"If we plan and budget carefully, we can run two households during the separation without too much discomfort."

Two households. Separation. We. So much in his statement to encourage hope. A thread still exists between them. With care, she can gather it, mend the rip. She must not act hastily.

"I'm going to the ladies' room."

Leaning across the sinks, Teresa examines her face in the mirror. Not beautiful, certainly not polished like an actress. Still basically flat, her stomach sways a bit over the sinks. Yet she can't deny a hint of crow's-feet at the eyes. How did she end up with neither youth nor money? It had seemed youth was a part of her fiber, her character, her personality, even her physical nature. She could not lose such a thing.

Teresa swings through the ladies' room door. The hefty blond hostess leans against the wall, drawing on a cigarette. The overhead light reflects on her blue glasses, concealing her eyes with white glare. Her hair, set wet, mimics the roller shapes. Teresa sees bobby pin lines, then notices a brilliant orange poppy embroidered on the woman's blouse: long orange stitches overlap one another, presenting the illusion of solid color. The image inspires Teresa.

"Are you the hostess?" she asks.

"Yes," the woman turns so her eyes appear behind the lenses. Watery blue to match her frames. The hand with the cigarette drops

138   G A R N E T T   K I L B E R G   C O H E N

to her side, as if the gesture will conceal it. She straightens, separating from the wall.

"I was wondering . . . It's my husband's birthday," says Teresa, the lie rolling easily off her tongue. "Could you have that group come to our table?"

"Sure," says the hostess, releasing her cigarette so it drops in a line to the floor; she crushes it beneath her heel.

"His name is Paul," says Teresa.

"So, why did you like the dog?" asks Teresa, pushing away her plate, lacing her fingers to fold her hands in the newly created space. Now that she has a plan, she feels relaxed. She recalls another movie, long ago, her hoody boyfriend, Kevin, pulling up his pants to sit in the theater, to prevent his knees from bunching. She sees the stretched wrinkles, midthigh, the way his knees sloped away, like twin mountain peaks descending into the darkness. She doesn't recall what movie they saw; only the image of his knees. The shiny navy fabric. In fact, she is startled to remember that the gesture was why she had broken up with him; it was too prim, too priggish, for him to retain the reckless hoody image she admired.

Paul's tight face slackens. She has disarmed him. He leans toward her. He almost looks animated. But what really touches her is the care he has given his appearance, the pains he has taken to look boyish and cool—his carefully tousled hair, styled to look out of place, his simple black jeans and T-shirt. Teresa wants to kiss his cheekbone. She has always loved his dark eyes, his high cheekbones, jutting from his mouth to points near his ears, like sharp scissor blades. In the corner of her sphere of vision, Teresa sees the hostess, stepping down the hall from the kitchen, carrying a plate aglow with candles. Waitresses and waiters trail behind the hostess.

"The way he appeared in almost every scene," says Paul. The parade of restaurant staff is practically upon them. Teresa's heart beats quickly. She squeezes her fingers. "Like a Greek chorus, giving the audience clues on how to read the scene, the significance, if he's asleep . . ."

"*FELIZ CUMPLEAÑOS!*" The staff surrounds them. Maracas rattle. Voices rise. A blur of color. The swing of skirts. The ripple of the waiter's sleeves as he shakes the maracas. A cocoon of brilliant fabric spins around them. Streamers of color. Teresa feels like they are the central pole in a May Day dance. A huge sombrero drops on Paul's head, slanting clownishly over his left eye. "Happy birthday to you! Happy birthday to you! Happy birth . . ."

"It's not my birth . . ." Paul sputters. A fried banana stuck with red candles is planted before him.

"Now, don't be embarrassed," says Teresa, a bubble of hysterical laughter rising in her throat. Bright colors continue to swirl past. Surround them. Red, yellow, blue, green, and pink.

" . . . to you! Happy birthday dear . . ."

The familiar red stain climbs Paul's neck. He starts to rise. The napkin drifts from his lap.

" . . . Paul, happy birthday to you!"

"*I said* . . ." Paul stands and rips the sombrero from his head. He flings it, so that it flops like a clumsy bird, across the room. It sails right above the heads of the people at the next table. "IT-IS-NOT-MY-BIRTHDAY!"

The wine-colored rage infuses his face. He glowers at Teresa, his eyes dark buttons, not seeing. He turns and stamps in the direction of the door. Teresa begins to rise, to follow him, but the pop of a flashbulb startles her into stillness. The waiter, abashed, drops the Polaroid in front of her and disappears. Teresa's eyes cloud, an effect of the bright light.

In the center of the table is a bowl of fake flowers. The blur of flowers transports Teresa back in time to her first Easter bonnet, a stiff white affair with a band of artificial daisies. Saffron pistils. Synthetic white petals overlapping one another. She remembers how the broad silk chin ribbon cut into her smooth young neck. She recalls her powdery white-gloved hands holding the handle of her first purse. The woven straw of her bonnet was so coated in glaze that the rim had cracked when she sat on it. And with the same lack of warning, she is back in Juan's.

Before her eyes, the details of the Polaroid begin to take shape. The scene sharpens into focus, a frame around them both, a smear of color between them, as if Teresa is snagged to the seat, a tangle of threads between her and her departing husband, unraveling them both as he pulls across the room. Her pale coral blouse and his black T-shirt pulling each other apart. She sees it like a perfect mise-en-scène, a frame around their unraveling life. She wants to ask Paul if he gets it? The fabric flashbacks she has been experiencing? Their life like a series of frames. Instead she hiccups and calls after him, "I just thought it would be fun." But he is already long gone.

Lost Women, Banished Souls

Darya and I stand in her kitchen. She leans over the stove stirring the contents of a huge pot; I sip from a tumbler of vodka. She and her husband, like my husband, are scientists, physicists; unlike my husband, they are also former Soviet refuseniks. Resembling immigrants of long ago, they arrived in this country with only a few boxes secured with crisscrossed rope. Here less than a year, they have already managed to buy this small house.

Many questions loom. Intellectual. Political. Cultural. Instead— so like me—I want to know how she has managed socially. Does she have friends? Women to talk to?

Resting the long wooden spoon across the pot rim, Darya steps away. She uses her hands to speak, opening and closing them, chin level, as if plucking American words from the air.

"I do not concern about friends. I see them like we are all molecules, how do you say . . . floating, we can connect and bind with certain other molecules, but not all. There is not room, the correct chemistry. But, also . . ." She looks up at her ceiling as if the right word might sail past. She has large mournful eyes circled in thick lashes, slashes of broad cheekbones, full lips. In spite of her lack of Western fashion sense, she is beautiful. She wears a flowered print blouse and a plaid skirt. Red patent leather shoes. " . . . it is not meaning if adhere to every molecule. Too many friends are not real."

She smiles at me, proudly, but also expectantly. She wants my reaction. She just attempted, in a foreign tongue, to convey a metaphor she has obviously long considered. I nod my head.

So soon after my breakup with Caroline—and though we are both straight women there is nothing else to call it—I want to understand why friendships end. How we lose people. I cannot stand to think of a broken thing, a lost thing, without possessing any power to immediately mend or retrieve it. I believe I can learn from Darya, a woman who has left everything she has known, every friend, to move to a strange country, bereft of all but her husband and young daughter.

The first friend I can remember is Patty. Patty-cake Patty, we would say and laugh playfully. In fact, her face was round, flat and doughy, like a pancake; her hair, pulled tightly back into a long ponytail, looked like maple syrup being poured.

We walked together to the bus every morning for kindergarten. Her sock cuffs were usually trimmed to match the hem of her skirt, the same lace or embroidery. Often we had cookies and milk together at her house after school (my mother didn't bake). I liked looking at Patty's round face while she ate. After each bite, she would lick the bite mark clean of crumbs before taking another. Her bouncy ponytail (my hair was cut in a pixie) bobbed up and down while she drank. Milk clung to the fuzzy down around her lips. After our snack, she would carry the plates to the sink and rinse them to stack on the sideboard. A strange custom. At our house, we left our plates wherever we ate. My mother collected them before a wash or when we ran low.

It was spring, I remember, when our friendship ended. Red tulip patches burst on either side of her front slab steps. Each bulb as big and glowing red as the glass candle boats on the tables at the Italian restaurant. Her mother opened the door.

"Is Patty ready?" I asked, averting my eyes. I was so shy that I didn't like talking to parents.

"Patty is sick today." Rather than respond, I ran down the steps, then the block, to the bus.

"Patty is sick," I told the bus driver as I clutched the sidebar, stretched my right leg the enormous distance to the bottom step, and climbed aboard.

An hour later, rain slid down the windows in great sheets. As we broke into reading groups, I noticed Patty standing by the coatrack, untangling her arms from her yellow-slicker raincoat. Over and over,

I see the image: Patty's arms emerging from the holes of her yellow raincoat.

I walked up to her just as she kicked off her second boot.

"My mother drove me. Why didn't you make the bus wait?"

"Your mother said you were sick."

Patty turned her round face on me in disgust.

"I was going to the toilet. What did you expect her to tell you?" she asked. *"That I was in the toilet?"*

"Of course not, Patty-cake!" I said, not certain how this was taboo. Why didn't my mother tell me these rules? These secret manners, rites of etiquette?

"And don't call me Patty-cake!" she said, stomping off to her reading group, the Silver Wings.

I never got to explain. Or even understand. An injustice was done to me, of that I was sure—but I'm uncertain about the precise unfairness. Was her mother wrong to lie? Or my mother not to train me in the little fibs people told? For years, I did not know. And then, once I realized it was perfectly fine to inform a caller that one was in the bathroom, I was positive that I must have remembered the story incorrectly—Patty's words, her mother's, could not have been what I recollected.

I almost had another friend in first grade. The opportunity passed so quickly that I wasn't prepared. I was standing in line waiting to be dismissed for recess when Gail approached me. With big buckteeth and bug eyes, her face was friendly. She wore a starched white blouse and a red and navy kilt.

"Do you want to play with me at recess today?"

Me? I wondered. I looked around.

"No, no thank you. Not today." The words came so fast that she was gone, on to another girl, before I realized what I had done. I wanted to slap myself. Why did I say no? Why? Why?

I spent recess sitting on a large rock behind a tree, spying on Gail and the other girl, her second choice, playing horse, galloping around the swing sets, tossing their heads back and whinnying. In preparation for the many times in my future that I would replay conversations, I went over and over my words to Gail. *No thank you. No thank you. No thank you.* At least I was polite. *Not today. Not today. Not today.* Did that leave me open for future recesses? Would she consider me again? I took comfort in the fact that I knew so little about horses that I never could have galloped or neighed as well as either of them.

Kit was my first lasting friendship. Tight braids protruded from her head like twisted pipe cleaners. Freckles spattered her nose. She looked innocent, rural, but was wicked. Not like Patty McCormick in *The Bad Seed* (our favorite movie), but a funny wicked, just short of cruel. The type of mean that made me laugh so hysterically I would sink to my knees crying, lose my voice in laughter, my breath. I would wheeze and wheeze.

She often snatched my last piece of candy from my hand and popped it in her mouth; hid my things (homework assignments minutes before they were due); put my mother's short blond wig on our dog (even knowing how hurt and angry my mother would be I laughed until I thought my belly would split); made hideously comical faces when I gave class reports, then acted outraged if I blamed her for my lack of decorum, but continued with the faces when the teacher turned away.

She was stronger than me and used her physical superiority against me. Though terrified of heights, I climbed many a tree and roof at her insistence; she even persuaded me to try Ferris wheels and roller coasters. (When I clutched the handlebars, she tried to pry my fingers loose.) Once she fed me a cat food and mayo sandwich. Another time she ran the hose through my bedroom window and greeted me with the twirl of the sprinkler when I entered. As the water sprayed my bed, my dresser, my beloved books and toys, I sank to my knees in laughter. Hers was a clever skill: Since she could make me laugh—even when under attack—I was never free to get angry with her.

Six Russian scientists talk with my husband in the living room, Serge among them. He has been in the States four years longer than Darya and her husband, has already secured tenure in my husband's department. Reportedly he is brilliant, the star of them all. By the time I join them, I am a little drunk on vodka. Otherwise I would never ask Serge's views on friendship. In that way I am sexist; despite the fact that both he and Darya are scientists, the question seems appropriate only for a woman. I try to explain Darya's theory; it tumbles from my mouth in an odd mixture of words. My husband looks at me perplexed. He is never embarrassed by my behavior, only curious. A true scientist.

I wish Darya would leave the kitchen to elucidate. I know little about molecules. So, with Caroline looming large in my consciousness, I attempt to develop my own theory. I say all friendships must end so we can move on. Serge interrupts. (That's a common trait among scientists, they never smile politely at one's stupid ideas, faux pas, instead they try to understand them, dissect them, or refute them.)

"Nonsense!" he bellows. At least he sounds a bit drunk as well. "When I left Moscow, I said good-bye to all my friends, my colleagues. We hugged. Final farewells. I never expected to see any of them again. I have seen them all, even my oldest high school friend is here in the States working at lab in California. The world is too small to lose people for good."

I have many friends I rarely see, perhaps a few times a year for lunch, a card at Christmas; other friends have faded away entirely. Yet none of these people feel lost. It is only the ones who disappeared while I was still very aware of their presence who seem lost. People who seemed cupped in my hands, then slipped between the cracks of my fingers.

Kit told me it was her or Kenny Kingsley, my first boyfriend, a hood with rich black hair swept back in waves from his sleepy eyes. Alabaster skin. Cheekbones like stones implanted beneath the skin. He wore tight black jeans, black boots with pointy silver toes. He was strong, could street fight, yet he possessed a sickly quality, a neediness. *Please, please, Kit,* I begged, *don't make me choose. I love him.*

I leaned against the wall of the auto shop where he helped his dad after school, wringing my hands. "No," she said, her lips twisted in a sneer, "I can't stand the way he puts his arm around you, like he's a drunk using you for support. Come with me now or that's the end of our friendship." She held her arms tightly crossed. No room for compromise. I glanced away. When I looked back, she was walking up Fordum Street. It was an unusually hot September afternoon, her image, separated from me by the veil of fumes from the body shop mixing with the hot air, seemed to waver, oscillate, behind the

LOST WOMEN, BANISHED SOULS   145

rippling pink-and-purple-laced air. If only she had made me laugh, she might have won. She could have said so much to make Kenny seem a comical figure, but for the first time Kit didn't use that tactic.

Every day when I came home, I asked if anyone called.

My mother's answer never varied, "Not a soul." I pictured Kit floating, a disembodied soul lost in the galaxies. In the future I would picture all my misplaced friends that way—for if they weren't in touch with me, surely they were lost.

For the rest of eighth grade, we passed each other in the halls without eye contact. We went to different high schools. I didn't see her again until my senior year when our schools played in football. I spotted her cutting down the bleacher row toward me, along the narrow footboard, people rising to make way. She must have seen me from the ground. She approached as if no time had passed since the day at the auto shop, taking up where we had left off. "It wasn't a normal hug, more like a wrestling hold. Like your head was part of his arm." I sat with new friends, the popular girls at my school— some of the ones to whom I still send Christmas cards. I didn't even introduce her to my friends. I looked at them, shrugged, and rolled my eyes, pretending I had no idea what this crazy girl was talking about. Kit would never know that the weight of Kenny's arm, her description of his hold, was why I broke up with him the summer after eighth grade.

Rosita. Rosita. Rosita. I loved her name, so different from those of my friends, my relatives. Rosita in her white cosmetology uniform. Her hair a shiny black bubble cut. Black marble eyes. Amber skin. Red-red lipstick. White-white teeth. Always laughing. A toothpick space between her two front teeth.

Rosita and her friends, all in white uniforms, crowded around the stainless steel drinking fountain in the vocational wing of our high school. Rosita's head thrown back, spraying water from the space between her teeth. A sparkling arch curving over the heads of her friends. More laughter. Water rising in a stream like the magic flow of a Greek fountain nymph.

Rosita and her hoody friends at the bus stop, smoking. A smoke plume curling up from Rosita's red mouth, French-inhale style, into her nostrils. Lips puckering so that the creases are burgundy, like the deep folds between rose petals, like her name.

Rosita laughing, always laughing. Rosita's ankle twisting, the toe of her cheap white sandal smearing the cigarette butt on the pavement. Rosita pulling another cigarette from her purse.

Rosita in her classroom, a mock beauty parlor, clipping the bleached head of a classmate. A thick ring of buttery yellow locks circling Rosita's white sandals. Rosita disappearing behind the partially closed door, reappearing with a can of spray, shaking it, a bobby pin clenched in her closed lips. Shaking. Shaking. Laughing, lips still tight around the bobby pin. Rosita's thin arm shaking from elbow to hand.

Rosita and her friends, a tight group, their bright dresses, bold adult hairstyles, staring straight ahead, clutching books to their chests, as they walked down one of the college-prep wings to a math class. A long, low wolf whistle. Boy laughter.

It took all my nerve to finally enter the girls' bathroom in the vocational wing: the cloud of smoke, the laughter and chatter.

"Can I bum a cigarette?" I asked a girl with orange hair. The laughter and talking stopped. Everyone looked at me. Quietly Rosita shook loose a slim white stick from her Marlboro box and passed it over the girl's arm to me. When no one offered a match, I took a pack resting on the sink and lit up. The red on the box in Rosita's hands matched her lips. No one resumed conversation. I noticed the bathroom was far more dilapidated than those in our wings. The sinks had not been replaced with modern ones. Broad sheets of dirty gray paint peeled from the walls.

The girl with orange hair locked eyes with mine. Her eyes looked different from those of my friends, not simply too much makeup. I couldn't place my finger on the difference then; now I know that though they were set in a young soft face, her eyes were as weary and hard as those of a much older woman.

Her thin orange lips moved.

"What the fuck's with you, anyway? You some kind of weirdo, Miss College Prep? Why does you always seem to be where we are all of a sudden? You best stick to your own part of the school."

Out of the corner of my eye, I saw Rosita turn away. I gave a quick— friendly, I hoped—smile and took a few more drags of my cigarette, tossed it in the toilet, heard the sizzle, and walked out the door. The moment the door swung shut, the noise resumed on the other side. Above the din, I could distinguish Rosita's rich and wonderful laugh.

LOST WOMEN, BANISHED SOULS

· · ·

In college I wanted to be Gwen. She wore large owl glasses, no makeup, and called herself a feminist. Curly white-blond hair rippled past her shoulders to form a point at the small of her back. She was only a few years older than the rest of us but seemed light-years ahead. She was divorced—had, in fact, escaped a violent husband in the dead of night—and was raising Phoebe, her little girl, by herself. They lived on food stamps and grants. Yet unlike the feminists our boyfriends mocked, she wasn't austere. Gwen had the power and beauty of a Gloria Steinem. She was small-boned and dainty with two huge brown eyes, one glass (her abusive husband had hit her so hard that the real one had dislodged). She usually had a wonderfully militant and handsome boyfriend, often one of our married professors.

In my junior year, Gwen's senior year, Caroline and I rented a house with another friend, Anne. Gwen and Phoebe lived next door in a run-down cottage. Neither Caroline nor Anne cared for Gwen. I remember Anne saying that Gwen couldn't be so smart or she wouldn't have married such a loser in the first place. Caroline criticized both the way Phoebe periodically played naked in the yard and Gwen's reliance on food stamps. "Great mother," she said, "and real independent!" Even though I thought Caroline and Anne unenlightened, I craved their acceptance. So I usually visited Gwen when they were away.

I loved to sit in Gwen's kitchen—the windowsill lined with potted herbs, framed prints on the walls rather than typical college posters—drink chamomile tea, and listen to her political theories and views. Her real eye always fixed on me intently while the glass one seemed off somewhere else, a place I could never go or understand. Those discussions, I'm sure, are why I changed my major from art to political science. And her eyes, I think, are why I never felt as close to her as I wanted. I longed to have her photograph on my desk, with the snapshots of my other friends circling my ink blotter; at times the framed faces seemed like a collection, at other times, an audience. The photos made me feel I could have them forever. But a natural opportunity to take Gwen's photo never occurred. This seemed to symbolize her attitude toward me: affectionate, but also dismissive—for not being serious enough, for not having lived enough.

During her last day in the cottage, Gwen asked me to baby-sit at 6 A.M. the next morning while she took tests for a special grant for graduate school. We sat on her porch watching two of her former boyfriends—their long ponytails twitching like those of wild horses—load the last of her furniture while we made the plans. Since her bed was in the truck, she was going to spend the night at a boyfriend's, but would be at my door at the crack of dawn with Phoebe. When Gwen and I made the final inspection of her empty house, I was overcome with both sadness and excitement. I was sad to see her home dismantled—dust balls rolling across the wood floors like miniature tumbleweeds, clean squares on the walls left by her prints, crumbs of dirt on the windowsills—but happy that Gwen seemed to want me in her future.

Right before she climbed into the truck cab, we hugged for the first time. *See you tomorrow*, she said, her hair hanging out the open window. *Good*, I said, *I'll get your new address then, and I want to get a photo of you.*

That night, Caroline's ex-boyfriend, a big stupid football player, came to the house drunk, screaming obscenities at Caroline. He squealed away in his father's car, shouting that he'd make Caroline pay. We called the police, who sent two officers to the house. I was surprised that they looked no older than us. They advised us to leave for the night. We went to the dorm, where we slept in sleeping bags on a friend's floor. Since I didn't know the name of the man Gwen was with, I couldn't call. It seemed pointless to leave a note because I took my alarm clock and planned to get up at five-thirty.

I have seldom felt so lost as when I opened my eyes to see the short hand of my clock on the nine, the long hand on the ten.

Caroline sat at our friend's desk, leaning forward applying makeup in a magnifying mirror trimmed with lights the size of Ping-Pong balls. She glanced at me in disgust and said, "Your fucking alarm went off at 5:30 A.M."

I ran home. No note hung on our door. No sign of Gwen or Phoebe. Panting, I leaped the steps to her unlocked cottage and quickly checked every room. The place seemed even emptier than it had the day before. Like no one had ever lived there to begin with.

I never saw or heard from Gwen again. But often I imagine the way she must have looked, Phoebe in her arms, the sky pink behind her. I see Gwen's real eye fixed on my kitchen door waiting for me to answer, her glass eye already dismissing me.

LOST WOMEN, BANISHED SOULS

• • •

Sylvia and I made quite a team, weaving between tables, trays lifted above our heads on spread fingertips so that our arms looked like those flat-topped African brush trees, laughing, never misplacing an order, confusing a drink. Though she had plain brown hair, hazel eyes, cheeks lightly pitted with acne scars, her name suited her. She *seemed* silver, *sleek*, the way she walked, talked up the customers, sipped champagne splits at the bar after we punched out. Laughed her dry Sylvia laugh.

It was my first summer after college, waiting tables on the Cape, my first job. Everything about the restaurant, The Sailors' Haven, seemed fun. For the first time in years, nothing of importance was at stake. No final exams. No possibility of failure. Even getting fired wouldn't have mattered; after all, I wasn't going to include the restaurant on my résumé. Maybe that's why I was such a good waitress right from the start.

The only waitress better than me was Sylvia, who had worked at the restaurant for over five years. Our skill granted us special privileges— to plan our schedules and never work food, only cocktails. Everyone else had to rotate. Cocktails was better, higher tips for less trouble. No waiting in the hot kitchen for orders to come up.

We flirted with the yachters, poured whiskey in the coffee we drank all night, sat at the bar sipping champagne splits after closing, went out to HoJo's for 4 A.M. breakfasts, then watched the sunrise on the beach where we talked about the men we liked, the other waitresses, and the general restaurant gossip. One of seven children, Sylvia was a "Jack Mormon," meaning she had fallen away from the church. Her family never talked to her except to beg her to repent. She told me funny stories about her brothers and sisters, growing up on a farm, the strange Mormon underwear her mother wore. She had me in stitches. But she never cracked up, only laughed that dry sardonic laugh and rolled her excess cigarette ash against the sand.

Summer became fall. Business dropped off and my tips began to wane. I knew I should compile a résumé or start applying for graduate school, but my life was comfortable. I liked the routine. Up all night, asleep all day. Then the manager we liked, Connie, was fired and her assistant, Tony, whom we all mocked—he was such a nerd, hung all the restaurant keys in a huge wad on his belt—was given her job. He said he saw her stealing from the cash register.

Looking back, I realize it was probably true. Divorced four times, Connie had a daughter from each marriage. Only one ex-husband paid support, yet Connie and her girls always dressed well and took expensive vacations. But at the time it seemed unfair—besides, she ran the place, why not take a little extra? It was the shove I needed to quit. I could resign with honor, in protest. I decided on the spur of the moment, marched into the kitchen, informed Tony he could find someone else, then told Sylvia as I punched out. An hour later she called.

"You were right," she said. "They shouldn't have done that to Connie just on one creep's word. I quit, too."

I was struck with guilt. *She needed her job.* She never would have walked out if I hadn't.

"You're a great waitress," was all I could say, more to reassure myself than her. "You'll find something else soon."

Fortunately she did find a job at one of the hotel restaurants. It wasn't as fun as The Sailors' Haven, but the tips were good and they had a health insurance plan. On the Friday of her first week, Sylvia asked me to meet her for drinks at the new place when she finished. She was working the lunch shift until she got the routine down.

She was alone at the bar when I entered, smoking, sipping her champagne. She laughed her dry laugh when she saw me. The sound rich with affection. I slid onto a stool beside her. She introduced me to the bartender and then asked about my job search.

"Oh, it's all right," I lied. I didn't want her to know that I wasn't even looking; I had decided to go to graduate school during winter semester. I was just waiting to hear on my applications. "I'm sure something will work out eventually."

"I've got a surprise," said Sylvia and smiled. Then she asked the bartender to go get the manager.

"What?" I asked.

"Just wait," she said, still smiling.

The manager, a tired looking woman in her late fifties, walked around the corner. She wore plaid wool pants, belted at the waist, accentuating her boxiness.

"This," said Sylvia, presenting me with a flourish of her arms, "is the one I've been telling you about."

LOST WOMEN, BANISHED SOULS   151

The woman looked me up and down, like merchandise. The pockets around her eyes were so puffy that I believed they might deflate with a pinprick. I can't remember the rest of her face.

"When can you start?" she asked.

"What?" I asked, honestly baffled.

"I got you a job!" said Sylvia, delighted with her surprise.

"If Sylvia says you're good, you must be," said the manager without a trace of joy. "And it's never easy keeping good people once the season ends."

When I picture the scene now, I see myself backing out of the room, shaking my head, *No, no, you've got the wrong girl, you ain't gonna find me waiting tables for the rest of my life.* Like a bad movie. Of course it couldn't have happened that way. It must have been worse. I must have declined politely, then sat drinking with Sylvia, both of us knowing not only that her surprise had fallen flat but also that I had never considered myself a waitress, like her, and that our friendship was ending.

I had a dream about Masha the other night. In it, she had amazing hair. Each strand was a different shape. Some stood erect like feathers; others were like thick blades of grass or flat and wide like leaves. In the dream, I loved her hair, envied it, until I came across her waking before she had a chance to straighten up. I realized it wasn't hair at all. The top of her head was concave so she had filled it with dirt and planted strange flora in it. She had a small garden growing off her skull. In the way that one can only do in dreams, I wondered why I had taken so long to notice.

If Sylvia was silver, Rosita red, than Masha was bright chartreuse. Day-Glo. She was my supervisor on the governor's campaign; I was her protégée. She taught me a lot. We were often working together until late into the evening. For an entire year we shared most lunches and many dinners. Without her, I never would have known who to trust. Nor, for that matter, ever have learned how to be properly paranoid. She was considered a brilliant political strategist. Only I knew that most of her crucial decisions were made with the I ching. Should the governor debate, even though he was the incumbent? Throw the coins! Is he better off being photographed at tennis or golf? Pull out that well-worn book and toss the coins! Funny thing was, I actually didn't think her behavior odd. When she was an hour late for an important fund-raiser, I simply nodded sympathetically when she said she couldn't leave because black bugs covered her telephone wire. And when she said she suspected her stylist mixed an evil magic potion in with her hair dye, I simply suggested she change beauty shops (come to think of it, that talk might have been the impetus for my dream).

Her breakdown seemed sudden to me. She fell to her knees screaming when we were filming a television commercial. I was taken aback. I had missed every sign. I guess that was why I was too frightened to visit her in the psychiatric ward. And why I made no attempt to look her up once she was released. At the time, I thought I was simply lost in the heat of the campaign. Then I convinced myself the neglect was due to the fact I had just met the man who would become my husband. He was an old college friend of my new supervisor. We were lost in our love: the political scientist and the scientist scientist. But now, when I think longingly of the I ching, recall how it felt to kneel on the carpet and invest all in the toss of the coins, I realize I couldn't handle seeing how much of me there was in her.

The incident with Caroline—the breakup that got me thinking of all my fractures with old friends in the first place—is still too fresh for me to know exactly what happened. When I repeat the story of Caroline to others, she sounds completely unreasonable. However, other people's support doesn't afford me much comfort. True, the facts make her look bad—but what about the rest? She was the only college friend I lived near after graduation, slightly less than one hundred miles between us. Once a season, we met for lunch or dinner, and every year or two spent a weekend together with our husbands. The rift occurred right before one of our quarterly lunches. Due to a forgotten dental appointment, I had to reschedule. When I called to explain, she lost it. She screamed and screamed, listing all my transgressions: two years earlier when I had forgotten her birthday; how I kept in better touch with other old friends; even gave me grief for spending so much time at that "weirdo Gwen's house" (how did she know?) in college. She accused me of never caring for her, of putting her up on a shelf (her words) and only taking her down when I needed her. Her argument wasn't fair. But I was so struck by the fact that I *had* recently moved her photo from my desk to a bookshelf that I was speechless. She confused facts; contradicted herself; and had *never* remembered *my* birthday. Despite this, I knew she was somehow right in spirit. How had she guessed that I considered her a second-tier connection? Unlike Patty, Kit, Rosita, Gwen, Sylvia, and Masha, I would have allowed her to fade gradually away. Ironically, her accusations gave her access to a more dominant place in my consciousness— the galaxy of lost souls—than she ever could have achieved otherwise.

After dinner, Darya shows me around her yard, the dry grass, two struggling rosebushes, more than they ever had in Russia. I notice that her neighbor's yard is all ground cover—myrtle, brick, and flagstone—except for the side strip between the house and the fence. An inch-deep trench, the entire length and width of this space, has been dug; a pile of bricks waits to be laid inside it.

"That's an interesting yard," I say. "No grass."

"An interesting woman," says Darya. "She's sixty-eight years old. After marriage for forty-five years, her husband leave her last year. She took back her unmarried name . . . how you say, surname?"

"Maiden name," I say. I feel a dull headache coming on, the beginning of a hangover. We both gaze over the fence into the barren yard.

"Ever since we move in she is covering the grass, removing it. It was beautiful, not dry like our grass. After forty years in the house, she starts now."

I turn to look at Darya.

"Maybe her husband liked the grass," I say.

Darya smiles at me, her huge brown eyes lock with mine.

"That's what I think," she says.

Our exchange transcends our occupational differences, our cultural ones, our language barrier. We have connected. We both know the moment is transient; our differences probably won't allow a permanent binding like the molecules she mentioned earlier, but I wonder if the very fact that our intimacy is fleeting could save her soul from banishment. Just as we link arms, and start toward her house, I catch—in my peripheral vision—a door open in the other yard. I don't glance over, but I can imagine the woman: stooped shoulders, wearing a print dress and broad-rimmed straw hat, carrying a trowel for smoothing cement. I picture her walking to the side of her house where the bricks wait, kneeling beside them, and starting to lay the groundwork, arranging and rearranging until she discovers just the right pattern to reshape and conceal all that came before it.

Acknowledgments

Special thanks to the Ragdale Foundation and the Virginia Center for the Creative Arts, where parts of this manuscript were written or revised; to Columbia College in Chicago, which provided sabbatical time to work on this book; to the friends and former teachers who read and commented on some of these stories; and to my husband, Fred, for his love, support, and computer expertise.

The following stories, some in slightly different form, have appeared elsewhere: "From an Eyelash," *Ontario Review*; "Cousin Rina's Return," *West Branch*; "Wrongs," *Descant*; "A Position of Trying," *Literary Review*; "Aunts," *Alaska Quarterly Review*; "Maps," *Other Voices*; "Appetites," *Chicago*; "Burying the Dead," *Westview*; "Where You Can't Touch Bottom," *American Fiction*.

About the Author

Photo by Bill Frederking

Garnett Kilberg Cohen's stories have appeared in such publications as *American Fiction, Literary Review, Ontario Review,* and *Descant*. Cohen is Professor of English at Columbia College in Chicago.